Exit Plans
for
Teenage Freaks

What Reviewers Say About 'Nathan Burgoine

Of Echoes Born

"Burgoine assembles 12 queer supernatural tales, several of which interlock…The best tales could easily stand alone; these include 'The Finish,' about an aging vintner whose erotic dalliance with a deaf young man named Dennis gets complicated, and 'Struck,' in which beleaguered bookstore clerk Chris meets Lightning Todd, who predicts his future wealth and romance. A pair of stories set in 'the Village,' a gay neighborhood, feature appealing characters and romances and could be components of a fine *Tales of the City*–like novel."—*Publishers Weekly*

"The best short story collections are treasure chests that sparkle—not from the gems they contain, but with a light greater than the whole as the reader is left knowing more about life. In such work the mysteries aren't solved, but the questions get redefined. And so the tales in *Of Echoes Born* shimmer like gold, and not the kind you'll covet. This is one of those books that, when finished, you hurry to buy copies for friends."—Tom Cardamone, Lambda Literaray Award–winning author of *Green Thumb*, *Night Sweats: Tales of Homosexual Wonder and Woe*, and *The Lurid Sea*

Light

"What's stunning about this debut is its assurance. In terms of character, plot, voice, and narrative skill, Burgoine knocks it out of the park as if this were his tenth book instead of his first. He, along with Tom Cardamone, has the considerable gift of being able to ground the extraordinary in the ordinary so that it becomes just an extension of everyday life."—*Out in Print*

"Burgoine's initial novel is a marvelously intricate story, stretching the boundaries of science and paranormal phenomena, with a cast of delightfully diverse characters, all fully nuanced and relatable to the reader. I honestly could not put the book down, and recommend it highly, as I look forward to his next novel."—Bob Lind, *Echo Magazine*

"*Light* manages to balance a playful sense of humor, hot sex scenes, and provocative thinking about the meanings of individuality, acceptance, pride, and love. Burgoine takes some known gay archetypes—the gay-pride junkie, the leather SM top—and unpacks them in knowing and nuanced ways that move beyond stereotypes or predictability. With such a dazzling novelistic debut, Burgoine's future looks bright."— *Chelsea Station Magazine*

"*Light* by 'Nathan Burgoine is part mystery, part romance, and part superhero novel. Which is not to say that *Light* emulates such 'edgy' angst-filled comic book heroes as the X-Men; if you'll pardon the pun, it is much lighter in tone."—*Lambda Literary*

Triad Blood

"'Nathan Burgoine is a talented writer who creates a fascinating world and complex characters...If you're a fan of demons, vampires, wizards, paranormal fiction, mysteries, thrillers, stories set in Canada, or a combination of the previously mentioned, do yourself a favor and check this book out!"—*The Novel Approach*

"*Triad Blood* was a fun book. If you're a fan of gay characters, urban fantasies, and (even better) both of them, you'll enjoy *Triad Blood*." —*Pop Culture Beast*

Triad Soul

"'Nathan Burgoine's *Triad Blood*, the first book in this series, was one of my favourite books of last year and *Triad Soul* is, if anything, even better...what sets it apart, and makes me genuinely love this book (and series) is the depiction, both in fact and in allegory, of queer community. The prose is generally crisp and cleanly written, but there are also flourishes of creativity that elevate the writing above the prosaic. It has heart, imagination, and skill. Like *Triad Blood* before it, I suspect this is going to be one of my favourite books of its year."—*Binge on Books*

"'Nathan Burgoine really excels at creating a fascinating and unique supernatural world full of interesting politics. If you are a paranormal or a suspense fan, I think there is a lot here that will appeal to you, particularly if you are looking for a unique take on the various supernatural beings. Burgoine has really created something engaging here and I definitely recommend the series." —*Joyfully Jay*

By the Author

Light

Triad Blood

Triad Soul

Of Echoes Born

Exit Plans for Teenage Freaks

Visit us at www.boldstrokesbooks.com

EXIT PLANS
FOR
TEENAGE FREAKS

by

'Nathan Burgoine

2018

EXIT PLANS FOR TEENAGE FREAKS

ISBN 13: 978-1-63555-098-6

This Trade Paperback Original Is Published By
Bold Strokes Books, Inc.
P.O. Box 249
Valley Falls, NY 12185

First Edition: December 2018

Credits
Editor: Jerry L. Wheeler
Production Design: Stacia Seaman
Cover Design by Inkspiral Design

Acknowledgments

Exit Plans for Teenage Freaks wouldn't have happened without so many people.

First, the entire crew of Bold Strokes Books authors, editors, and lesser-praised-but-intrinsic members of the publishing team who were there at the retreat in Easton Mountain where a fun pitch contest turned into an idea that wouldn't leave me alone. Nell Stark and Jennifer Lavoie, especially, both of whom gave me "that look" when I said I couldn't imagine trying to write a YA given my own youth experiences. And, as always, Jerry L. Wheeler, who takes what I write and hands me back an edited version that makes me guilty to take the credit.

Second, the four high school groups—be they called SAGAs, GSAs, or Rainbow Clubs—who let me ask questions and listen and be included in some amazing, and often hilarious, conversations. I have never felt so much hope in my life, and I will never forget the hysterical pan-bi "clarification" discussion of 2017. I hope its inclusion here will give you all a chuckle. Also, I hope I did a good job with the Rainbow Club, specifically peopled for you amazing young people with your awesome bow ties, indomitable will, and seriously brilliant insights.

Third, my ASL buddies who didn't let their fluency slip like I did, my former ASL teacher, and my interpreter friends who really helped me with trying to find the balance in print. Highest praise and my eternal thanks to Scott Patrick Tozer, who went above and beyond, and I hope the namesake clearly illustrates my gratitude. At this point, I'll also note any mistakes made here in any way relating to ASL are totally my fault; it's a language with its own syntax and grammar and idiomatic style, and my own imperfect understanding is the culprit, not the experts who donated so much of their time to help me.

And, of course, to my husband, Dan. I couldn't do any of this without him. If I could open a door to anywhere? He'd be on the other side, every time. Unless he's watching another mathematics YouTube video.

Hey you, setting up the board game? Scribbling stories, drawing characters, watching sci-fi, rolling dice, placing meeples?

I see you.

To-Do

- ☐ Bring home calculus textbook
- ☐ Exam prep: calculus, biology
- ☐ Exam prep: English (reread?)
- ☐ Exam prep: French (practice exam!)
- ☐ Movie night with Alec this w/e?
- ☐ Make lunch for Tuesday, slacker

ONE

On the list of things I'd considered might go wrong in the last two weeks before I had finals, it hadn't occurred to me to put "teleporting to the aviation museum" among them.

But here I was. At the museum.

The guy behind the ticket counter probably wondered why I'd just walked into the museum and stopped dead with my mouth open. I was wondering the same thing, but not in the same way since just a few seconds ago, I was many kilometers away at school.

"You okay?" he asked, which made me realize just how long I'd been standing there.

"Yep. Yes, I mean. Yeah." I was nodding so fast I must have looked like a bobblehead. I took a deep breath, trying to calm myself down. Sweat broke out across my forehead. I felt woozy, like I'd just run a small marathon. I didn't do marathons. Hell, I tried to avoid running at all, unless maybe someone was chasing me.

This was *impossible*. I was standing in the aviation museum. I could see the gift shop and the cafe and the Lancaster Bomber and it just wasn't possible, but here I was.

What the hell had just happened to me? Had I snapped and gone completely mental? Maybe I'd get an upgrade in nicknames from Colenap to Colesnap.

I shuddered.

The man was frowning at me again.

Make a plan, Cole. That was my thing. I was good at it. Plans, I mean. Not getting stared at. Although, truth be told, I was pretty good at that, too.

Move. Rather than stand there with my mouth open, I made my way into the gift shop. The guy at the admissions desk finally went back to what he was doing. Immediate crisis averted. Except not at all. Because, again: *museum.*

I rubbed my temples, shaky and not just a little bit dizzy. Maybe I was sick. Did I eat something funny?

Plusses and minuses. Plus? The longer I stood there trying to calm down, the better I started to feel. Minus? The museum didn't stop being a museum. I looked at the rack of postcards in front of me without really seeing them.

Okay. Think. *How did you get here?*

No idea. One second I was at school, the next—

Wait. Was it the next? Had I lost time?

Was it like before?

Oh God, anything but that.

An older woman stood reading a book at the cash register. She hadn't seemed to notice me, which I was fine with. I circled closer to her, and she looked up and smiled.

"Hello," she said.

"Hi," I said, looking at her monitor. The clock and the date was in the bottom corner.

I exhaled in relief. Nope, that was right. No lost time. Same day, same hour, same impossible location.

Lunch will be over soon. How am I going to get back to class?

"Are you okay, dear?"

"Awesome. Great. I mean, I'm good." I smiled at the woman, going through the lobby again and refusing to make eye contact with the guy at the ticket counter. I pushed my way through the glass doors to the outside.

The aviation museum was basically in the middle of nowhere, off the highway where an old airport had once stood. No one could see me, so it didn't matter if I just stood for a little bit. It was a nice day, and the air helped clear my head.

Other than feeling suddenly bone-tired, I was very much my usual self.

What, exactly, had just happened to me?

❖

It was a regular lunch. We were sitting at our usual spot outside near the field on the front rows of the bleachers, talking. Rhonda had her head in Lindsey's lap, and they were taking pictures of each other with their phones. Grayson was texting one of the ever-shifting possible new boyfriends he kept talking about and laughing just loud enough at whatever he was writing or reading to make us look over at him now and then. Nat had their eyes closed and face turned up to the sun, and I had my bullet journal open and was sketching everyone's faces into the spaces around my latest to-do list.

I had no idea my day was going to take a detour into the surreal. These were normal things. Lindsey and Rhonda were always being super-sweet to the point of giving the rest of us cavities. Grayson always wanted us to notice what he was doing. Nat was always miles away from the rest of us.

I always made lists and then drew all around them.

Finals were coming, and my list was mostly my study plan. I wanted to ace French, didn't have too much fear about my English exam, and was working on when to go over my calculus and biology notes.

"Why did I take calculus?" I said. I was currently holding on to my B+ by the skin of my teeth.

"Because you're smart," Nat said, without opening their eyes.

"I'm not smart."

"You're smart," Nat said again, in that frustratingly confident voice they had.

"Tell that to my B+."

"Some of us would kill to have a B+ in a math class," Grayson said.

"Some of us could, if they'd study now and then," I said.

"See?" Nat said. "Smart."

I put down my notepad. "I don't even need calculus."

Nat finally opened their eyes. "How do you sign math?"

"Two M's. Like this." I showed them the sign.

They smiled. "See? It might come up. You might need to interpret calculus for someone."

I blinked. I hadn't thought of that.

"You just gave him something new to worry about," Lindsey said.

Nat laughed. "I did, didn't I?"

"No," I said, though I wasn't sure I meant it. "I'm good." I wasn't good. They were right. It was one thing to look ahead at an interpreting career, but it was another to realize once again how many different concepts I still had no idea how to work with.

"I'll be right back," I said. "I just want to get my phone and check something." We weren't allowed our phones in class, and I hadn't stopped to pick mine up at the start of lunch. I'd bought my lunch today and wanted to get to the cafeteria before the line had gotten too long.

"You worry too much," Nat said, but I just shrugged and put down my notebook and pencil.

I didn't worry, exactly.

I just thought a lot about possibilities. Contingencies.

And interpreting calculus hadn't been a possibility I'd considered before.

This wasn't the first time I'd faced vocabulary I hadn't known. All last summer, my dad had let me shadow him on his video remote interpreting business, and a guy had booked an appointment to talk to the aviation museum. I'd taken a tour of the place and realized pretty quick I didn't know how to sign a crap-ton of engineering terms. My dad walked me through doing my own research. I'd spent a couple of days there beforehand, reading the plaques and using my phone and my computer to figure out creative ASL interpretations for words like "aileron" and "variometer." After he'd done the official tour, we'd come back the following week and done a pretend version of our own with him as the "client" and me interpreting, and it had gone pretty smoothly.

Maybe Nat was right. Maybe doing enough homework did make me smart. They were definitely right about being prepared for new topics.

I reached for the door to the school and pulled, thinking about all the stuff I'd learned about the Lancaster Bomber.

And then…

Poof.

❖

Was that it? I looked warily at the door to the museum. I'd been thinking about this place. And here I was.

Should I click my heels?

I closed my eyes and thought about school. The grey brick, the glass front, the library, the computer room, my friends, our spot on the bleachers. Hell, I even thought about the office and cranky old Mr. Bundy.

But when I opened my eyes, I was still right here. Light-headed, a bit woozy, but definitely still at the aviation museum.

Okay, now what? I needed to get my butt back to school from kilometers away without freaking anyone out, and that was going to involve someone who didn't mind bucking the system and who maybe wouldn't ask me any questions if I begged them not to.

That left one option: Alec.

I reached into my pocket for my phone and groaned.

My phone was in my locker. *Right.*

I closed my eyes and tried to think. My brain felt like it got when I forgot to look up and realized just a few minutes of Tumblr had turned into hours. I took a few deep breaths, but it didn't help at all. I was definitely off. I wasn't exhausted, but my body was definitely...heavier. I just wanted to lie down for a second.

Maybe I'd left behind some brain cells at the school.

New plan.

I didn't have many options. I just needed a decent story. Someone was supposed to meet me, maybe. I'd go back inside and ask the guy at the front desk if I could borrow his phone. I could say my ride was very late.

Worst the guy could do was say no, right?

"From now on, get your damn phone before lunch," I muttered. The pizza hadn't been worth being first in line, and how hard would it have been to stop by my damn locker before I went?

I pushed at the door to the museum.

And it happened again.

Poof.

Two

Wherever the hell I was, it was dark, cramped, and I barely fit. When I tried to straighten, I hit my head on something and the hollow metal clash it made was so familiar, it clicked. I heard a variation on that sound so many times in a day I would recognize it anywhere: it was just like someone slamming a locker door.

I was in a locker.

I sagged against the tight metal walls, feeling dizzy and weak. Was I going to pass out? I felt even more trashed than I had just a few seconds ago at the museum.

I closed my eyes and tried to breathe through it. One or two breaths' worth of fresh air in the locker were with me, and then after that the smells of the bright day outside the museum were gone, and all I got were the scents of the locker itself.

Which was shoes, mostly. Gross.

Once I managed to twist around, I saw light coming from the metal slats at the top of the door. And on the inside of the door, I could see a couple of photos and magnets and a whiteboard...

My whiteboard. *My* photos. *My* magnets.

I was in my own damn locker.

Well, at least I knew the combination.

Fat lot of good it did me from *inside* the locker, though.

Simple plan: get help, get out of the locker. This time, my phone was close enough to make that happen.

Reaching behind me, I tried to find my hoodie. It was hung up on the hook, and if I could find my hoodie I could get my phone from the pocket.

I managed to get my hand into the pocket, but it was a tight fit what with me being shoved up against it. When I pulled out my phone, it came free with a jerk and clattered to the floor of the locker somewhere between my feet.

Of course.

I tried to shimmy down, but I didn't have enough room to bend my knees. I couldn't get my hands low enough in the confined space.

I was trapped in my stupid locker. At any moment, the damn bell for lunch was going to ring and then what was I going to do? I'd have to kick and scream to get someone's attention. Everyone would stare. Austin and his idiot friends would laugh. People would whisper about me every time I walked past for the rest of the school year.

Again.

"Goddamn it!" I yelled.

"Hello?"

The voice made me jerk my head, which hit the hook where my hoodie was hanging, which made me swear.

"Hello?" A guy's voice. Someone was in the hallway.

I took a deep breath. My choice was public humiliation in front of the whole school, or private humiliation in front of one person.

No contest.

"Hey." I raised my voice. "I'm stuck in a locker." I rattled the door.

"Whoa." Now that he was closer, the voice sounded familiar. Then again, it wasn't a huge school. Whoever he was, though, at least he wasn't laughing.

Yet.

"Yeah," I said. "It's my locker, though. If I tell you the combination, could you, like, let me out?"

"Uh. Okay."

"Eleven, forty-three, fifteen."

The sound of the guy turning the lock was louder than I expected from inside the locker. Thankfully, he got it on the first try.

When the door opened, I tried to step out gracefully, but it was hard to crouch and duck my head and lift my feet high enough. My left foot got caught on the edge of the locker, and I went face-first into the guy's chest. He caught me, which was lucky, and he was strong enough that I didn't knock us both to the floor, which was even luckier.

"Careful," he said.

I'd thrown my arms around him, but now that I was out from the locker, I got my feet back under me and let go, stepping back.

And that's when I realized I'd just gotten rescued from my locker by Malik King.

Because it wouldn't be my life if the cutest damn guy in school hadn't just witnessed my humiliation.

❖

"Are you okay?" Malik said. I wasn't sure if we'd ever had a conversation before.

"I'm fine," I said. *I seem to be teleporting, but other than that, I'm solid.* I managed what I hoped was a decent smile. He stared at me. He had great eyes. Dark brown, but with little flecks of gold in them. Good lashes, too.

Malik frowned. I was staring. Shit.

"I just wanted my phone," I said. It came out in a blurt. I cleared my throat. "Thank you. For..." I waved my hand at my open locker.

"What happened?" Malik asked.

Good question.

I turned my back to Malik and bent down to get my phone. Maybe by the time I turned around again, he'd be gone, and I wouldn't have to come up with some plausible reason I'd been trapped in my own locker.

No dice. He was still there. Also I had two text messages from Grayson asking me where the hell I was and how long did it take me to get my damn phone.

"Cole?" he said.

Wait. Malik King knew my name? I let the little thrill in my chest play out a couple of seconds before I squashed it. Of course he knew my name. It wasn't like we had a thousand students. We'd even shared some classes in the last few years since his family had moved here. Also, he was on the same basketball team as Austin. I should probably just consider myself lucky he hadn't called me the other thing.

"Yeah?" I said.

"Who put you in your locker?"

Oh shit. Well, no sane person would assume I'd willingly locked myself inside. I mean, how would that even work? How would you close the lock?

"It doesn't matter," I said.

His crossed his arms, opened his mouth to say something else, and then I was literally saved by the bell, which rang above us.

My phone buzzed, too.

Another text from Grayson.

Nat has your stuff. Weirdo.

Any second now, people were going to start filling the hallways, coming in from the cafeteria and outside.

"Thank you," I said. "I mean it."

Malik looked like he wanted to say something else, but then he shook his head and walked away. I watched him go. My jeans never fit me like that. The world was an unfair place.

I shook my head. Man, I could barely stand up straight. My legs felt heavy. As the rest of the student body showed up, I reached into my locker for my biology textbook, turned around, and made it three steps before blackness rushed in from all sides, and I fell over.

This time? No one caught me.

❖

If there's a way to face down your dad when you've got a split lip that doesn't make you want to crawl into a hole, I don't know it. In fact, I was pretty sure I was going to burst into tears, which was totally not what I wanted to do. I wanted to get out of there as fast as possible with whatever shreds of dignity I had left.

One of the best things about having a dad who's basically a professional reader of body language? He got it. Right away. He took one look at me and signed, *Want go home?*

I nodded, hard.

"I'll take him home," he said to the nurse.

"It might just be his blood sugar," she said, speaking far too loud in the small room. Lots of people did that. It was never not annoying. But my dad read her lips and smiled his crooked smile.

"Got it," he said.

That was it. I was sprung.

The nurse had given me a juice box I'd sucked back while they'd called my mother. She must have texted my dad, who was much closer to the school since he worked from home, and he'd gotten there pretty fast. On a really nice day, I could walk to school in about twenty minutes. Dad had gotten here in less than five.

Me mess up your work? I asked once we were out in the hallway. My hands were still shaking. I didn't speak. I didn't trust myself to talk without bursting into tears.

He shook his head. *Have twenty minutes break! Then more work.*

That was a relief. Some of the hearing interpreters Dad worked with had booked their sessions weeks in advance, interpreting for really important things, usually over the computer through group video chats, but sometimes in person. He once drove three hours to interpret for a funeral, and he often team interpreted for a doctor talking with Deaf patients. He had contracts with a lot of organizations.

When he got to the car, he turned to me, face-on.

Lunch, eat finish?

"Yes," I said, finally trusting I could hold my shit together. "I just got really dizzy. The nurse says that can happen, though. I got up too fast, maybe."

My dad frowned at me. One of the worst things about a dad who's basically a professional reader of body language? He can tell when I'm not being completely honest.

Seriously, it's totally brutal.

What happened?

I didn't know what to say. I mean, I couldn't tell him the truth, right? No big deal, Dad. I teleported to the aviation museum, and then when I tried to come back, I ended up in my locker. I think the almost-fainting had something to do with that, but I'm not really sure because I might be having some sort of incredibly bad hallucinations, or maybe I've lost my mind. Oh, and I finally said more than two words to Malik King, but only because he got me out of my locker.

Yeah. That wasn't going to fly.

But looking into my dad's eyes, there was no way I could lie. This was my *dad*. He was, like, the jackpot of dads. He always took time to make sure I was doing okay and seriously seemed to care if I wasn't. Okay, he told terrible jokes. Dad jokes reach whole new lows when you can add ASL puns, but he was more patient than anyone I'd ever known. He and my mom were basically a walking, talking life-goal for the kind of relationship I wanted some day, even though my plan involved a husband, not a wife. Heck, even the gay thing? Model parenting, which was more than I could say for some of the rest of the Rainbow Club.

Grayson's dad had taken months to be okay with his kid being gay, but my dad had opened his arms right on the spot and offered me a hug. It was perfect. After, he told me he'd already noticed how I looked at other boys. Again, professional body-language reader. It had made me supremely self-conscious, but the hug at the time was pretty awesome.

I had to say something to him. He had dad-face, and dad-face would not be denied.

I settled on a very, very literal—but not at all illuminating—truth. *Don't-know*. In ASL, it's one sign.

He put his hand on the back of my neck, giving me a little squeeze. It helped, though it made me want to bawl again.

I'm pretty sure he noticed, because he faced forward again, turned on the car, and then we were on our way home.

❖

Predictably, my phone started pinging the moment I lay down on my bed.

From Lindsey: *Did you really collapse in the hallway?*

Rhonda: *Answer Lindsey. She's worried.*

Nat: *Let us know you're okay, okay?*

Grayson: *Gravity sucks.*

I sent back quick messages to all of them saying I was okay, but I was going to take a nap. I asked Rhonda if she'd mind letting me know what we covered in biology class, which we shared. Then I turned off my phone, plugged it in, and grabbed my big grey sweater. It didn't see life outside my room. It was one of my dad's old university sweaters, and even though I wasn't cold, I pulled it on and lay back down on my bed. Comfort sweater, activate. I closed my eyes. I'd catch up on whatever we covered in class, and maybe a nap would do me good after my dose of insanity and public humiliation.

No doubt everyone was already talking about it.

Did you hear?

Colenap passed out in the hallway.

What a freak.

Patterns of light moved across my eyelids. My lip hurt where I'd bitten it. I curled up on my side and took a deep breath, my brain spinning too much to fall asleep, no matter how wiped I felt. I didn't feel quite so dizzy anymore, which also helped. No matter how much I tried to dismiss what had happened as some sort of hallucination, I didn't think it was.

Which meant…

I opened my eyes. It took way more effort than it should have.

Which meant I'd been at school, and then the museum, and then inside my locker. All within a few minutes. It wasn't possible, but it had happened.

I sat up. My dad was downstairs in his office, but he'd be starting his meeting any minute, so I couldn't talk with him. Also, if I told him what I thought had happened, even the best dad in the world would be taking me back to Dr. Macedo, and that was absolutely not a path I wanted to explore.

Not yet, anyway. I mean, if I was hallucinating? Then, okay, therapy was definitely the way to go.

But I wasn't. I was *sure* I wasn't.

I'd been there. And there was no arguing about being in my locker.

I picked up my phone again, sitting on my bed so I didn't have to unplug it, and sent a text to Alec.

You got a second to talk?

The reply came almost instantly.

Sure. Heard about your day.

Nothing like public humiliation to really wrap up the year, eh?

You passed out?

Not quite. I sort of fell down. Bit my lip. It's attractive.

Hey, chicks dig scars.

I don't dig chicks.

Life is pain, princess.

I smiled. Trust Alec to work in one of our favorite movies. This was exactly what I needed. Alec was the coolest guy I knew, and my best friend. If anyone would be able to handle my insane story, it would be him. But could I tell him?

I typed in: *You free tomorrow after the meeting?* and then hesitated.

Before I'd decided whether or not to send the text, another message popped up from him. *Seriously, though, you okay?*

I blew out a breath and hit Send on my text.

Sure. Talk then?

Talk then.

Okay, see you tomorrow.

Kisses, I sent.

I felt better already. I leaned back on my bed, wondering if maybe I should get up and find my biology textbook. I closed my eyes. That felt better. My brain might have been going a mile a minute, but my body was heavy. And honestly? Biology could wait.

I fell asleep.

To-Do

- ☐ Bring home calculus textbook
- ☐ Exam prep: calculus, biology
- ☐ Exam prep: English (reread?)
- ☐ Exam prep: French (practice exam!)
- ☐ Movie night with Alec this w/e?
- ■ Make lunch for Tuesday, slacker
- ■ "What happened?" joke
- ☐ Laundry

THREE

Tuesday morning, I took a deep breath and told myself I would make it through the day. Breakfast had been as normal as it ever was at home, the typical routine being my mom and I falling behind and running late because no one in my family can resist our snooze buttons. The kitchen had been chaos with three of us on a deadline. My dad had an early VRI call, so he'd barely waved and swallowed some coffee before he changed into a shirt and a tie to sit in front of his computer.

He wasn't wearing pants, but you can't tell that sort of thing on a webcam.

My mom and I were even more of a mess, despite Dad making us packed lunches. By the time I'd run out to the roadside to catch my bus, half a piece of toast in one hand, I'd not really allowed myself to think too much about what had happened on Monday. Even my mother had barely tossed a "you feeling better?" my way as she dashed out the door, which had made it easy to not think about it.

I mean, okay, the split lip was a bit tender and really, *really* ugly, but so long as I avoided reflective surfaces, maybe I could get through the whole day without thinking I had lost my mind. Instead, I threw together a quick addition or two to my to-do list on a piece of paper in my pocket. I even had a joke prepared.

Then I got to school and found myself face-to-face with my locker. Right. That.

My hand was shaking so hard it took me two tries to dial the combination. When I finally opened it, a slick oily feeling dropped into the pit of my stomach.

My calculus textbook had a footprint on it. Also, the thin metal shelf was dented. That was new, and pretty much shaped like the top of my head. My photos were crooked, the little whiteboard had slid halfway down the inside of the locker door, and the week's plan was all smudged.

So. That made it official.

It wasn't a hallucination.

"Here you go."

I jumped, and Nat stepped back, blushing.

"Sorry," they said. They were holding out my stuff from yesterday.

"It wasn't you." I took my books, my bullet journal on top. "Thanks for grabbing this."

"Are you okay?" They had on a long, black button-down shirt with a cool lime-green bow tie. They had a whole collection of bow ties. They also had the habit of looking at me like they could see right through me. Nat reminded me of my dad sometimes.

"Low blood sugar isn't sweet," I said. "Apparently it's what makes all the cool kids pass out."

"Uh-huh." Nat's frown made it clear they weren't buying it, but they didn't press. "You coming to the meeting today?"

"I'll be there."

They nodded and gave me one more long look. "You're sure you're okay?"

"It's my lip, isn't it? It's ugly."

"It's not so bad."

"Oh my God, what happened to your face?" Grayson said, joining us.

Nat sighed.

"I bit my lip when I fell down," I said. I wanted to put my hand in front of my mouth. "Low blood sugar is not sweet." I wagged my eyebrows.

"What?" Grayson said.

"Sweet. Sugar?" I said.

"You shouldn't try to be funny," Grayson said. "It's not really your thing." He put his hands in the pockets of his skinny jeans and sort of *posed*.

"Leave him alone," Nat said.

"Oh wow, that looks super-painful."

I turned. Oh, hurray. Lindsey and Rhonda were here now, too. It was the complete rainbow set except for Alec, but he hadn't been much for completing this particular set lately.

"It doesn't really hurt." Much.

"You should tell people you got into a bar brawl," Grayson said.

"Except lots of people saw me face-plant right over there," I said, pointing.

Grayson looked. "Do you think anyone got it on video? We could make a gif. You could be a meme."

Oh God. Was that possible? Of course it was. I groaned.

"Stop talking, Grayson," Lindsey said.

"What?" Grayson said.

The bell saved me from more humiliation, and we broke up for our homerooms, Rhonda and Nat walking with me. We took our seats, and I noticed a few stares right away. God, I hated that. I ducked my head down a bit, pretending to be really engrossed in whatever I'd written in my notes yesterday. I hated it when people stared. I'd had a lifetime supply of that already.

Mr. Jones took attendance, and then the announcements came on. I listened with only half an ear—I so didn't care about the last rally game of the season—and then glanced out the window at the field. Only instead of looking out the window, I noticed Malik King was watching me.

I glanced down again. Yep, those notes were *super* interesting. Certainly as interesting as Malik's brown eyes. And way more interesting than the way he could crook his right eyebrow up like he'd done. Maybe he was looking past me, at someone behind me. I looked up again.

Nope, his eyes were still on me. He repeated his little eyebrow-rise thing. The smile was gone, though. Instead of friendly, he was looking at me like maybe I was about to faint again or something. God, he was cute.

Not for the first time, I wished I had instincts. There's a reason I'm a planner. My bullet journal might be *totally* nerdy, but when stuff happens and I'm not ready for it, I have no idea what to do. Like, say, when the cutest boy in the freaking class is looking at you and doing the eyebrow thing? There's a response that doesn't make you look like a complete moron.

People with instincts know what that response is.

People who plan? We do not.

I nodded at him and tried to smile in a way that said, "Hey, look at me, I have instincts and they are good."

He frowned.

I flashed him an okay sign. That, at least, wasn't open to interpretation.

Down to literally days left in this school, and no one cared to remember me at all. That was fine by me.

Until now.

Because I passed out.

Because I *teleported*, and then passed out.

Colenap was back on the radar.

Mrs. Salisbury started talking, and everyone settled down. I stared straight ahead and tried to listen.

I told myself it didn't matter. I should just let it go. Like every adult in my life had told me, I could choose not to let what other people thought bother me. I had two weeks left, plus exams. Once they were done, I'd never have to be in this room again.

No matter how many times I said that crap to myself, it didn't matter. How do you *let go* being considered a freak? There's no letting that go. Not when you've got people like Austin willing to remind everyone. Not when one face-plant in a hallway is enough to resurrect interest in the school freak.

I fingerspelled the word. *Freak.*

Head down. Grades up. Graduate. Leave. I'd made it this far. I could do another couple of weeks.

When I got out of town and made it to university, "Colenap" was going to be a thing of the past no matter what it took.

❖

I grabbed my lunch—and my phone—and headed off for the field behind the track. The last thing I wanted was company, but it wasn't possible to be alone indoors at school. Well, it was, but only in an "alone in a crowded room" kind of way. Still, the field behind the track was a pretty close second, with a row of large trees where small groups of friends gathered most nice weather days to eat. I was quick enough to claim a tree of my own, sat back against it, and exhaled. You couldn't see me from the bleachers, which was the goal.

"Hiding?"

I jumped. For a loud guy, Grayson could be quiet when he wanted to. He grinned at me.

"Not hiding, exactly," I said. "More like wallowing. But you can join my pity party if you want."

Grayson sat beside me. He had a giant container of pasta. How he was so little blew my mind. I'm not tall, and I didn't get my dad's shoulders, but beside Grayson, I didn't feel quite so tiny. He popped the lid, swallowed a forkful, and leaned over, bumping my shoulder with his.

"Why wallowing?"

"You want the list alphabetically or chronologically?"

"A is for assholes? B is for blood sugar?"

I couldn't help it. I smiled. Grayson was an idiot and had zero filters, but he could always make me smile. When I didn't want to punch him. "And C is for Colenap. I got Colenapped again today."

Grayson winced. He'd recently bleached and dyed a really dark purple streak into his black hair, and he'd pierced his ear again, which I think meant he now had a half dozen rings in his ear. I kept meaning to count, but Grayson never sat still long enough.

"Sorry. That really sucks," he said finally. He seemed honestly sympathetic. Grayson was hard to read. He moved all the time, but it didn't always feel *honest*. My dad had taught me a lot about body language and nonverbal stuff, but Grayson muddied the waters. I was pretty sure he did it on purpose.

I shrugged and took a bite of my sandwich. The lettuce crunched, and I was pretty sure I had real mayonnaise and tandoori chicken. My dad made the best sandwiches.

"You seem more out of it than usual," Grayson said, pausing to swallow. "No offense."

"None taken." Grayson had no idea how right he was about that. Not dwelling on Colenap was one thing. Not dwelling on maybe losing my mind or maybe *teleporting* was another. "Out of it" was as good a descriptor for deep, deep denial as anything else. "I guess." I took another bite.

"Who Colenapped you? Was it Austin?"

I looked at him. Grayson had a tight look on his face, and he was stabbing his fork into his pasta like it needed to be punished.

"Did he say something to you?" I asked instead, worried.

"Oh, he's not that dumb," Grayson said. "Well, no, he's a fucking idiot, but he learned after last time. He just stares. Or he 'bumps' into me. Always says sorry, but, y'know."

I did know. Austin got suspended last year for a week for dumping a cup of pop down Grayson's back. He tried to play the accident card, but between zero tolerance and bad luck on his part—Mr. Jones had seen it happen—his so-called defense was tossed out the window. Ergo, suspended. Austin hadn't done anything obvious since then. Instead, he'd gotten *subtle*. Well, as subtle as Austin could be. Especially with Grayson.

Part of that? Grayson stood out, and not just because of the earrings and the hair, either. He seemed to do it on purpose, despite how much negative attention he sometimes got. That day Austin got suspended, Grayson had come to school in his "Real Men Kiss Men" T-shirt. It hadn't gone over well with quite a few of Austin's crowd, but only Austin had been dumb enough to go too far.

Sometimes I wondered if Grayson was only being true to himself, or if he really just wanted to pick a fight.

"You want to tell Nat?" I said.

"Do you?" Grayson said. "You're sure you just fell down?"

Ah. There it was. The reason he'd tracked me down.

"It wasn't Austin," I said. "Not today and not yesterday. I really did just pass out."

He stabbed some more pasta. Then he sighed. "Two weeks."

The countdown mantra to the end of the year. I held out my fist. He bumped it.

We ate in silence for a bit.

"It's just…it'd be so *him*, y'know? Trip you up," he said. "You're *sure* it wasn't Austin?"

"I'm sure," I said. "Let it go, Elsa."

He grunted. "Too bad. I would love to have him kicked out just before graduation. Maybe he'd have to re-do a whole year."

I grinned. "You're vindictive. I like that about you."

"I'm down with vengeance. It's my best quality."

"No way. Your best quality is your optimism and faith in humanity."

He laughed so suddenly he choked on his lunch. The other kids at the other trees stared as I whacked him on the back until he coughed up some pasta.

Okay. So high school wasn't entirely bad. Maybe I'd miss a few things.

"Jerk," he said, once he recovered. "I keep telling you, don't do jokes. Not your thing."

I finished my sandwich and looked across the track. Someone was standing there, looking right at us. Not a student, an adult. He had a beard, and he was wearing a suit. I didn't recognize him, which was weird.

My stomach clenched, an old and entirely unwelcome reflex I wished I didn't have. Stranger Danger. Some days I wondered if I'd ever recover from a knee-jerk reaction to spotting someone who didn't maybe belong where they were. It was stupid. I was totally safe. Heck, Grayson and I were surrounded by students at every one of the trees along the field, but some rando staring in my direction across a field?

It gave me the squicks.

"Who's that?" I said, giving in to the feeling.

Grayson glanced up and looked where I was looking.

"I don't know. A sub, maybe?"

The man turned and walked back toward the school.

My heartbeat returned to normal the moment he'd turned his back on us. I took a couple of deep breaths.

"You okay?" Grayson said.

"No," I said, shrugging. "Of course not. Have you met me? I'm a complete freak."

"No more than any of the rest of us," he said, going back to his pasta. It might have been meant as a joke, but I heard the feeling beneath it. Grayson was a good guy. An annoying, loud, *incredibly* frustrating good guy, but a good guy despite it all. And maybe he'd nearly ruined almost everything when he'd decided Alec was the one, but...

But really? He *was* just like the rest of us. Looking at him now, it might have been the way the sun was showing off the purple streak in his hair, or it might have been the way he was stabbing at his food, but it occurred to me maybe the person Grayson wanted to pick a fight with was himself.

You're worth love, I thought. A shiver spread across my skin. I rubbed the goosebumps off my arms.

He frowned, glancing over at me. "What?" he said.

"Just thinking."

"On second thought? I take it back," he said, but unless I was mistaken, Grayson was blushing. "You make lists. You like studying. You actually *know* what you want to do with your life. I think you're sort of the biggest freak of all of us, y'know?"

I laughed and went back to eating. I glanced up a few more times before the bell rang, but the man didn't return. Grayson was probably right. Just a sub.

So why did I feel so anxious?

"All of the thoughts," Lindsey said, coming to life. She was the most social and outgoing of the whole group. "Head into the city?" She sounded hopeful. "Dance our asses off?"

"Do we want to do that again?" Rhonda said.

"Last year *was* pretty awesome, and I'm not saying we have to do something different," Nat said. "Also, Ottawa Central started a new club, too, so more people could show up this time."

"Didn't their guy reach out to us in September?" Lindsey asked.

"Ryan," Nat said. "Yeah."

"Well, we can ask them all for feedback, maybe? But we should ask Central to come," Lindsey said.

I liked the sound of that. For the last three years, our little club had connected with a network of GSAs, PFLAG groups, and rainbow clubs from the high schools in Ottawa, gathering to have a "we made it!" party. Six clubs were pooling our resources—which were pretty scant—but it had been fun. Ottawa Central made seven. Last year, the Kanata group had gotten us a bar for the night. They didn't serve us, of course, and it had been a private event, but we had music and dancing and it had been pretty cool to have, like, an actual crowd of us. Best thing since Pride, frankly. Also, there was this really hot guy in the Kanata group I *so very nearly* got up the guts to talk to. Maybe this year, I could think of something clever ahead of time and actually say something to him.

"Don't forget Kanata," Grayson said.

Hm. Great minds.

"Will you do the speaking?" Nat asked me.

Aw. I grinned. "Of course. Just let me know what you want to cover." Nat was our font of knowledge, but if any of us needed to stand up at the front of a crowd and speak, it usually fell to me. Lindsey hated doing it, Nat said it made them want to hurl, no one trusted Grayson not to offend everyone, and neither Alec nor Rhonda had ever even suggested they might want to try it out.

Me? I loved public speaking. Give me a topic, time to plan, and a lectern? I'm your boy.

"Would you maybe do something along the lines of your speech from English?"

"It was epic," Grayson said. A compliment from Grayson? Man. I knew the speech had been good. I did my independent study unit on non-inherited cultures. It was called "Born to Those Who Aren't Like You." To say it was the best thing I think I've ever done in school would still be understating it. Mr. Jones made me promise to rework it into an essay submission for some bursaries he knew about. Like, actual cash could come my way from that speech.

"I can do that," I said. I was pretty sure I was blushing now. "I can drop some of the Deaf stuff, make it even more queer."

Nat nodded. "It's a great speech, and it's a good way to remind everyone to connect with the other clubs. Keep the lines open. It's a great networking opportunity."

"Says the machine," Grayson said. This time it wasn't so much a compliment. "Some of us just want to have a good time with other fags."

I winced.

"Sorry," he said, raising his hands, though it didn't sound entirely sincere. "Other *queers*."

I shook my head to show him I didn't mind—except, well, I did. I hated that word. After a pretty relentless hounding in grade eight by a couple of Austin's douchebag friends, I wasn't sure I'd ever be up to reclaiming the word. That was how Nat always put it: "reclaiming." And it was funny, because I totally got "queer." But then again no one had ever shoved me into a wall and called me a queer, so…

The door opened.

I'd like to say we all turned with polite smiles on our faces, ready to welcome whoever was coming a little bit late to the club meeting. That was a huge part of the group's purpose, after all. We were supposed to make everyone, allies or queer people alike, feel like they were in a safe space and welcome to join us.

In reality? We all pretty much gawked.

Because Malik King was at the door.

"Hi," Nat said, recovering first, because of course they did.

"Hi," Malik said. He hesitated.

"Come on in," Lindsey said. "We don't bite."

Grayson opened his mouth, but Nat and Rhonda both elbowed him. They had good instincts.

"Ow," he said, instead of whatever he'd been about to say.

Malik paused a second longer, then came in and closed the door behind him. He looked good, but he always did. And it was really annoying, if I was being honest. I mean, no one should be able to make a T-shirt and jeans combo work the way he did. It was probably the shoulders. When you had shoulders like Malik King, T-shirts just fit the way they were supposed to.

He also had a great chin, dark eyes you could totally forget the world in, and as far as I could tell, his brown skin had never even considered a zit, which was cosmically unfair. When he took one of the empty seats in our circle of chairs, he nodded at me, and I realized I was staring. I forced myself to look back to Nat.

My face was burning. I wondered exactly how bad my lip looked. It suddenly felt giant and swollen and gross. It probably looked disgusting, too.

Chicks dig scars, Alec had said.

I wondered if Malik did.

"Welcome," Nat said. "I don't think you've been to one of our meetings before, so let me quickly go over the guidelines. This is a totally safe space. Anything said here stays here. Also, if you don't know the right words to use, just use whatever you think will get your point across, and we'll take it in the spirit intended. We'll help provide the language after, because words matter and part of what we do is help people speak respectfully of other people. We ask you to respect our pronouns and names." They softened. "But if you get it wrong, just try harder next time. None of us are here to judge or assume, and if you don't want to say anything, that's all right, too. We're just going over planning an end-of-the-year party, and then we'll open up to new topics."

Malik nodded. He was super polite. "Okay."

Having Malik in the room seemed to affect everyone differently. If anything, Nat got even more formal, and their discussion of potential party places ended up sounding like we were deciding on our very own second-prom or something. Lindsey, on the other hand, went from her usual upbeat self to something close to a cheerleader, and Rhonda—always the quiet one—didn't say a word.

Grayson, for his part, was sneaking glances at Malik whenever he could. Which was what I was doing. At one point, we met each other's eyes, and I could practically hear Grayson's voice screaming in my own head: *Malik King is at the Rainbow Club!* I swear he was vibrating down to the roots of his purple streak.

"I wish we could try something different," Rhonda finally said, breaking her silence. "Don't get me wrong, I like music, and dancing's cool, but we've done that every time."

"Maybe we could ask one of the Ottawa Village pubs if they'd let us have a trivia night," Lindsey said. I could tell she'd much rather stick to the music and dancing, but she was trying to support her girlfriend. It was sweet.

"If they're licensed, we'd have to figure out a wristband option or something like last year," Nat said. "Or maybe do it on a night they don't stay open, if they have one."

"Have you guys done a group game thing before?" Malik said.

Everyone stared at him, and at best I'm pretty sure we were all skeptical. Grayson especially had an expression that said, "Dude. This isn't gym class."

I felt bad for Malik, and I didn't want Grayson to say something out loud so I said, "What kind of game?" I hoped he didn't mean we should all go watch a football game or something. Lindsey did gymnastics and I wasn't the world's worst skier, but that was about it for athletes among the Rainbow Club.

"Last year, for football, we did glow-in-the-dark bowling." He shrugged. "It's more fun than it sounds. And it's different."

Nat made a note. "I'll put it on the list for the other clubs to look at."

No one had any real suggestions after that.

"Okay, anything else?" Nat said.

"Uh," Malik said, and once again everyone was looking at him. The guy had guts, that was for damn sure. Probably guts came free with every purchase of gorgeous forget-the-world brown eyes.

"Go ahead," Nat said.

"I just wondered what you guys were going to do about Cole being locked in his locker."

Oh shit.

No one was looking at Malik anymore. No, every single person there, Malik included, was staring right at me.

To-Do

- ☐ Bring home calculus textbook
- ☐ Exam prep: calculus, biology
- ☐ Exam prep: English (reread?)
- ☐ Exam prep: French (practice exam!)
- ☐ Movie night with Alec this w/e?
- ☑ Make lunch for Tuesday, slacker
- ☑ "What happened?" joke
- ☐ Laundry
- ☐ Slap Malik King

FIVE

I t's not…It wasn't…" I said, desperately trying to figure out a way to head this off before it began, but that's as far as I got before Grayson was talking over me.

"Who the fuck shut you in your locker?"

"Grayson," Nat said. "Let him talk."

I took a deep breath. I really didn't have the slightest clue what to say. I couldn't tell the truth. I mean, I *could*, but then they'd think I was insane.

Frankly, *I* was still fifty-fifty on whether or not I was insane.

I opened and closed my mouth, rejecting everything I could come up with before I started. I probably looked like a fish, complete with a ripped lip from a freshly removed hook. I couldn't think of a single thing to say.

I wished Alec was here.

"You don't have to talk about it if you don't want to," Rhonda said. I had never been as grateful for her soft voice as I was right that very moment.

I nodded at her.

"Not if someone *put him in a locker*," Grayson said. "We need to know." He was angry. Of all of us, he was the one who'd suffered the most bullying over the years. Heck, for most of us, high school had been awesome. We were riding a wave of zero tolerance, and stuff like getting shoved into lockers just wouldn't fly here. But Grayson knew how much "zero tolerance" could just turn *out loud and obvious* into *quieter and meaner*. "Was it fucking Austin?"

"No," I said, because it *wasn't*. Now what? I stared down at my hands.

"Sorry," Malik said. I looked back up, and it's possible I glared at him. Jackass. What the hell did he think he was doing? Saving the gay boy? To his credit, he looked really uncomfortable. He bit his lip. "I thought you would have told them."

"Apparently not," Grayson said.

If I was really, really lucky, maybe the earth would open up and swallow me whole.

"I'm really sorry," Malik said. "I should go."

He stood up, and his movement finally knocked my brain back into gear.

"No," I said. "No, don't. I…" I took another long breath. "I don't know," I said. "I don't know what happened." My stomach twisted. It was the truth, but would they believe me?

"You didn't see who did it?" Grayson said. His voice had finally lost that angry edge, and he almost sounded gentle.

"Do you want to go to the principal about it?" Nat asked.

What I wanted was for everyone to stop staring at me.

"I—" I said. "It's just…there's nothing I could say." That, at least, was the truth. I felt like crap. I didn't want to let people think some homophobic asshole in the school had shoved me into a locker. Bad enough Malik thought so, and now the rest of the club. I didn't want the whole school thinking something had happened when it hadn't. God, if any teachers caught wind, they'd make some announcement or force people into some sort of discussion. If a split lip was going to resurrect Colenap, the story of me being crammed into a locker would bring it back forever.

The whole group was silent. Grayson was clenching his jaw. Nat was tapping their pen against their notepad.

"I'm not going to put it in the minutes," they said. "And we go by the club rules. This stays with us. Confidential." They looked at Malik. "You, too."

Malik nodded. He was still standing there, awkward and embarrassed. He glanced at me. The look on his face?

Pity.

That was it. The humiliation box had been colored in. I was *done*.

I grabbed my bag. "I'm going to go. You guys finish without me." I was moving before they could protest. Both Nat and Grayson said my name with varying levels of frustration. I wanted to be anywhere else but here, especially somewhere Malik King wasn't looking at me with his super hot brown eyes full of freaking pity. My whole body seemed to pull itself out of the room, like something had anchored itself in my chest and was now reeling me in.

Anywhere but here.

I pushed my way through the door.

And it happened again.

❖

The tinkle of the bell was familiar, and despite the unreality of it, it only took me a second to realize I was not at school anymore.

I was at Meeples. I'd just come through the front door of my favorite store. Shelves of books lined the far walls, with little chalkboard signs above each one telling you what was where. The store carried mostly fiction. At the front half, tables and the shelves were full of board games. I came here all the time. It was empty right now, which was a little unusual, but any of the kids from school who might be on their way probably wouldn't have made it this far yet. Meeples was just off Main Street. It was too far a distance to cover.

Y'know, unless they teleported.

"Shit," I said.

"Cole?"

Candice was standing behind the counter, working her way through a box of books.

I forced myself to smile. My heart was hammering in my chest. Again. I couldn't believe it had happened *again*. "Hi."

"You okay?"

"Uh." I swallowed. "Yeah. I…Yeah. I'm fine." Strangely enough, I even meant it a little bit. The more I looked around, the more I came down off the sudden shock of being here. I loved this place. Candice decorated the place with all sorts of nerdy stuff. She had a little Harry Potter closet under the stairs that went up to where she kept the kids' books and did Sunday readings. X-wings and TIE fighters hung on little strings from the ceiling near the sci-fi section. Touches like that were all through the store, and she'd stenciled quotes on the walls, too.

In fact, I was staring right at "Curiouser and curiouser." Preach, Alice. Preach.

But if I had to fall through any rabbit holes, Meeples was maybe my favorite place to land. If that made me a huge geek, that was fine. Candice was amazing at finding me books and games I'd like, and I often dragged Alec or Grayson or Lindsey here for coffee and fun, especially after our club meetings. It had become kind of a thing. Lindsey was a Settlers of Catan shark.

"You must have booked it from school," Candice said. "No one else with you?"

"I left Rainbow Club early," I said.

I didn't normally have such an easy time lying. I should probably worry about that.

She paused, looking over her glasses at me. "Everything okay with your friends?"

"Yeah, they're good." I really wished another customer had been around. I finally got my feet moving and made my way to the counter. "I just felt like some alone time."

"I'm honored," she said, with a little smile. "Onirim?"

It was a solo card game where you played as someone trapped in a kind of endless dream where things made no sense.

So, y'know, I could relate.

"Sure," I said. "And, uh, I'll have a hot chocolate." At least this time I had my phone and my wallet with me. And my bag. Though, really, it was only a twenty-minute walk home. I could have done way worse.

Like, say, the aviation museum.

I sat down. I felt a little off, sort of heavy in my hands and feet, but it was nowhere near as bad as the last time. That was…good? Bad? I had no idea, but at least it wasn't worse. I felt a little light-headed, but I didn't feel any sign of the headspins from a few moments ago, and though I'd pretty much crashed into a coma last time, right now I just felt a bit tired.

Candice brought me the box, and I started shuffling the cards, mostly for something to do and to stop my hands from shaking. I pulled out my phone, putting it on the desk beside me, and dealt myself a starting hand. The goal of the game was to collect keys and find your way to the right doors to get out before you ran out of time and were lost forever. I drew out my starting hand, and I got a door right away. I'd have to shuffle it back in, since the doors were the goals and you couldn't start with them…

Something clicked when I saw the card.

I turned around and looked at the entrance to Meeples. I'd heard the bell when I got here. The door had closed behind me. I'd been leaving the music room, my hand had been on the door, and I'd ended up here.

I'd been going through a door at school when I'd ended up at the museum.

And when I'd tried to go back into the museum, I'd ended up in my locker.

Doors.

I stared at the card.

It was *doors.*

My phone buzzed. It was Alec.

Where you at?

Crap. I'd totally bailed on him. I'd told him we'd meet after the meeting. I'd kind of hoped he'd be there, though I wasn't surprised he hadn't shown.

Sorry. Left the meeting. Long story. I'm at Meeples. I'm an idiot, sorry.

I can be there in fifteen.

I was so grateful I could have cried. Instead, I just sent him a text: *Kisses.*

I put my phone down and started the game. I found all the doors I needed before I'd even made it halfway through the deck. That had never happened before.

I decided it was a good sign.

SIX

The door opened about fifteen minutes later. A sick surge of anxiety rushed up into my stomach, and I turned to see it wasn't Alec after all, but a man who was maybe in his thirties. He was staring straight at me and didn't seem too pleased I was looking right back at him.

"Sorry," I said, when he didn't look away. He had a kind of bumpy nose that made me think it had been broken. "Waiting for someone. Thought you were going to be my friend."

"May I help you?" Candice said, and I turned back around again.

"Coffee," the man said. He didn't say "please," which annoyed me on Candice's behalf. I watched him. He didn't look like the sort to come to Meeples, which didn't often attract the suit-and-tie crowd. Candice's greeting had been cordial and professional.

That probably meant she didn't know him.

I sighed and turned off my Stranger Danger alarm. The man might be rude, but he just wanted a coffee.

I went back to my cards. My second game wasn't going anywhere near as smoothly, and I was pretty sure I wasn't going to be able to pull off a win. The next card I drew had the little monster on it, and I eyed the deck of remaining cards.

Yeah. No way. Time to throw in the towel. No need to drag it out. The threads of anxiety in my gut loosened.

I shrugged, shuffled the cards back together into one big pile, and started putting them back into the box. To my surprise, the guy in the suit—and it really was a nice suit, sort of a charcoal grey, with a black shirt and a red tie that was the only real splash of color—had sat down and was tapping away on his phone, his coffee so far untouched.

He caught me looking at him, and I smiled.

He looked away.

Well. So much for community outreach with the suit-and-tie crowd. I had a brief, weak moment of wondering if the man could tell I was gay, then shrugged it off. Who cared? This was Meeples. If some random stiff in a suit didn't like me on sight, I could cope.

I pulled out my bullet journal. My daily to-do list was officially in tatters. I hadn't studied, though I at least had my calculus textbook in my bag, since I'd grabbed it from my locker before the meeting. In fairness, "teleport to Meeples" wasn't on the list either, so it hadn't been part of the daily plan.

I doodled a quick sketch of Candice in the margin. Her hair was a challenge. She almost always wore it braided, and I'd yet to get it right. Today was no different.

The door opened again. This time, it was Alec.

The relief I felt was palpable.

Alec was wearing jeans and a grey sweater. He was a big guy, wide-shouldered and stocky like his dad. He'd needed to start shaving in eighth grade and had more or less given up by the eleventh. He always looked tanned, even in winter, which was unfair, but his skin had been hit harder by the acne fairy than me. It was fading now, and if it was possible for a few acne scars to be attractive, that was how it played out. The overall result was scruffy, but it worked for him. I pretty much thought of him as my walking, talking teddy bear.

Something I could never, *ever* tell him.

I got up, and he gave me one of his awesome hugs. The last of my nerves melted away as I felt him squeeze me before he let go.

"Hi, Alec," Candice said.

"Hi," Alec said, letting go of me.

"Mocha?"

"Thank you. You read my mind."

We sat down, and he eyed the Onirim box on the table. "Please no."

I laughed. Alec wasn't big on board games. "It's fine. I already played two solo rounds."

He exhaled. "Good." His phone pinged. He checked it. "So, that's the third person to ask me if I know where you went in the last ten minutes."

I took a swallow of my now not-so-hot chocolate instead of answering. It was almost gone.

"Ah," Alec said. "You're avoiding them."

I put down my cup. "Sort of?" Did it still count as avoiding your friends if you accidentally teleported away from them after a public humiliation? Probably.

"Was it Grayson?"

I shook my head. "No. It wasn't Grayson. It's not always Grayson."

Alec snorted.

Right. Well. Last year's mess was a whole other mountain to climb.

"I just…" Once again, I wasn't sure what to tell him. I didn't like this feeling. At all. I usually knew what to say. It was, like, the only advantage of constantly imagining conversations that hadn't happened yet.

"Is it about the locker?"

I scowled. "Meeting stuff isn't supposed to leave the meetings. And you don't come to the meetings anymore."

Alec crossed his arms. He was big enough to pull off the intimidation look. "You want me to kick someone's ass?"

"There's no one's ass to kick," I said.

He frowned.

"Look," I said. "I can't rat anyone out. It wasn't…" I sighed.

"You didn't see who it was, did you?" Alec said.

Here we go again. The same assumption the club was making. And it was tempting to take the out, but I didn't want people thinking I'd been stuffed into my locker by a non-existent homophobe at school. I didn't want people looking at me—once again—like I was damaged goods. The freak. The kid who got shoved around.

Colenap.

I closed my eyes. I didn't have a strategy for dealing with this. I had run through all sorts of imaginary encounters with potentially hostile idiots in my life. My folks had been so endlessly overprotective that I'd finally gotten them off my back by begging them for self-defense classes. They'd jumped at the idea, and I'd even passed the courses with flying colors. I wasn't dumb. I didn't go places without telling them, I didn't ghost on my friends, and I didn't leap before I looked.

I was a planner. Planning was the only way I'd gotten any freedom at all.

But this shit? There was no plan for this.

"Cole." Alec squeezed my hand. I had a weak and selfish moment of wishing he was just like me, but he wasn't. I'd come to terms with that last year when he'd come out at Rainbow Club. Alec was ace.

"I'm okay," I said. "I refuse to let this become a thing. It *can't* be a thing."

He didn't look happy, but he nodded. Alec knew me better than anyone in the club.

I exhaled. If I had Alec in my corner, I could handle anything. He squeezed my hand again.

"Okay," I said. "Help me figure out how to tell them all I don't want to do anything about the whole locker thing."

Candice brought Alec his mocha, and when he thanked her, I glanced up and saw the guy in the suit-and-tie was looking right at us. For a second, I almost let go.

Instead, I held Alec's hand until the man looked away.

Take that, hater.

❖

"Are you sure you won't come?" I said. "Have my back? You know how they can get about standing up for ourselves."

Alec didn't have a poker face. He grimaced. "Really? You think having me there would help?"

"Grayson can be a complete dick," I said, "but he doesn't speak for all of us, and if I'm going to face them and tell them to drop it, I'd rather not stare down their 'we're not mad, we're just disappointed' faces on my own." I gave him my best puppy eyes. "Please?"

Alec groaned. "You're relentless."

"It's part of my charm."

"Is that what you call it?" He shrugged. "Sure. Okay. One meeting."

It would have been heroically uncool to punch the air in victory, so I held back. Just. I had a plan and a wingman. Life, as they say, was good. Bring on Thursday.

We gathered our stuff, and I paid for our drinks and brought Onirim back to Candice. Alec put his arm over my shoulder and gave me another squeeze, and I couldn't help but glance to see if suit-and-tie man was going to react, but he was gone. The table he'd been sitting at now had a couple of kids I recognized from school, playing a game I didn't recognize.

We made our way to the front of the store, and I nearly tripped us both up when I stopped just a step short of the door.

Right. Doors.

"What's up?" Alec said.

"So, it's possible I'm developing a door phobia," I said.

"What?"

I forced a smile and gripped the door handle, hyper-aware of everything around me. I just wanted to pass through the door and end up on the street. A normal thing normal people did with normal doors. I felt the door give, felt the cooler air outside against the back of my hand, and then my face. I heard the sounds of the street outside.

There was...something. A...*tug*?

Go. Just go.

I stepped through.

And nothing happened. I was on the street.

Alec followed, and he touched my shoulder.

"It's okay if it threw you," he said.

"Pardon?"

"The locker. It's okay if you're freaked out a bit about it. Really."

He didn't know what he was really talking about, but that didn't mean he wasn't right. I was indeed freaked out. And more than a bit.

"Thanks," I said. "Hey, any chance you can give me a ride home?"

"Of course," he said. Then he blinked. "Wait. Did you walk here from school?"

I shrugged. *Watch the amazing planner* not *lie by not answering the question at all.*

"Dude," he said. "Did you run? You were here pretty fast."

"I got here like that," I said, and I snapped my fingers.

He shook his head. "I'm parked over here."

❖

"So. Was it just the locker thing?"

Alec's Jeep was a lot like him. Big, maybe a little dinged up, and super comforting. It smelled like him, too: a combination of coffee and something vaguely sweet. He worked on it at his dad's garage and had pretty much fixed it from a barely running piece of junk into a perfectly good car even if it maybe still resembled one that wasn't.

I faced him. "Sorry?"

"Last night. You said you wanted to talk, but we didn't really talk."

Oh. Right. "We talked."

"Uh-huh." There was no doubt about how much he believed me. Crap. We didn't often do this whole "talking about our feelings" thing, but I wasn't going to get out of this easily.

I supposed I could just blurt it out. But the more I tried to figure out a way to bring up my teleportation, the more my chest tightened. I caught myself staring at Alec, his big shoulders and his scruffy hair and his surplus jacket that looked like it was going to fall apart at any minute, and I just couldn't get my damn mouth to work.

He glanced at me. "It's okay," he said.

"It's really not." I exhaled.

"When you're ready. I get it. Just…you're okay, right? You'd tell me if you weren't okay?" Man, he always could see right through me.

I couldn't get the words out, so I nodded. Even with Alec so close, I couldn't bridge the gap. He might as well have been on the other side of the river. Somewhere far away.

Like, say, the aviation museum.

Thinking about my trip sure didn't help my mood. I closed my eyes and imagined telling Alec. *Hey, Alec, it turns out I can teleport. You got any secrets you want to share?*

"Pardon?" Alec said.

Shit. Had I said that out loud? "Hmm?"

Alec shook his head. "Thought you said something."

We pulled up in front of my house.

"I'm okay," I said. I even meant it.

Alec's smile always made me feel better.

"We're overdue for a movie," he said.

"Truth."

"We'll figure it out."

"After Thursday, maybe? I think I'll have an open social calendar after that."

"Don't underestimate them. Y'know, except for Grayson. Grayson will no doubt live down to your expectations."

I rolled my eyes. Those two.

Alec didn't pull away until I was at my front door. I waved. Once his Jeep was out of sight, I put my hand on the door handle, then let go like it might bite me.

Doors. They were everywhere, once you thought about it. What with buildings and stuff.

Just like before. Just focus on staying where you are. You're going home. Going through the door into your own home is easy. This is where you live. You're not going anywhere.

By the time I opened the door, I had myself completely convinced it was going to be fine.

You'd think I'd learn.

Poof.

To-Do

- ■ Bring home calculus textbook
- ☐ Exam prep: calculus, biology
- ☐ Exam prep: English (reread?)
- ☐ Exam prep: French (practice exam!)
- ☐ Movie night with Alec this w/e?
- ■ Make lunch for Tuesday, slacker
- ■ "What happened?" joke
- ☐ Laundry
- ☐ Slap Malik King
- ☐ Doors? DOORS!
- ☐ Alec at RC on Thursday

SEVEN

The good news was I was home.

    The bad news was it was the wrong one.

Don't let anyone else be here. Please don't let anyone else be here.

The new owners of the house I'd lived in until I was ten had repainted the entrance hall a soft yellow. It was nice. Sort of cheerful. Did cheerful yellow-paint people freak out when teenage boys showed up in their homes unannounced? The coat rack didn't have any coats on it. Maybe that meant I wouldn't have to find out.

The dizziness passed while I stood there, breathing. Even faster than the last time.

Okay. First thing, get the hell out of here. Preferably unnoticed.

I turned around, grabbed the door handle, but it didn't budge. Locked and dead-bolted.

The organized part of me filed that away as interesting information. Apparently, I could teleport to the other side of a locked door. The rest of me tried not to notice how much my hands were shaking as I undid the two locks and cracked the front door. No one was outside.

I was a good half-hour walk from where I wanted to be. We'd moved when my dad's business needed an office, but neither my mom nor my dad had wanted to leave town, despite my campaign for us to move to Ottawa or Toronto or *anywhere* that wasn't where Colenap loomed over my head.

Still, a half-hour walk wasn't so bad, right? I mean, it was lucky we hadn't moved to Toronto after all. How in the world would I have gotten back to Toronto from here?

The same way you came.

I froze, hand still on the doorknob.

You need a plan. You need to stop doing this at random.

These were facts. How long before the incredible teleporting freak ended up somewhere *really* unfortunate? My locker was bad enough. There were worse options. Public ones.

I let go of the door.

So. Was there a plan to cover this?

Ignore it and it will go away? I didn't even sound convincing in my own head.

I took a long, deep breath. *The same way I came.*

Home, I thought. Specifically, my own, *current* home. Where my stuff was, where my mother and father were. I pictured the front porch, and the lopsided light fixture my father had installed just shy of straight. I thought about the breakfast bar we all often ate at, despite my mother swearing to use the dining room more. Then I pictured my room, my bed, my desk.

I stepped through the door.

Poof.

❖

I was either going to dance or burst into tears.

Maybe both.

I was in my bedroom. *My* bedroom, in *my* house. I pumped my fist in the air.

"Yes!"

The effect was maybe a little lessened by the way my voice cracked, and it's possible I had to wipe my eyes on my sleeve, but success is success, and I wasn't going to ruin my own moment. Teleportation. I could do this. I just had to put figuring out this whole teleporting thing on the to-do list, right between calculus and biology. Totally. I looked at myself in my mirror.

"You're so screwed," I muttered.

"Cole?"

I jumped. It was my mom. I whirled around, but my bedroom door was closed, which again struck me as something to remember.

"Yeah?" I opened the door.

She was still wearing her dental hygienist outfit. She had a ton of different patterned scrubs. Today it was butterflies.

"I didn't hear you come home. You made me jump."

"Sorry."

"Your dad's making dinner tonight. You want to help?" She stretched, raising her hands over her head. I heard the little pop her neck made.

"I will do that."

"Okay. Shower time for me." She looked wrecked. We both got those really dark smudges under our eyes if we were tired.

"Long day?"

She nodded. "No empty units, no no-shows, and an angry mother who blamed me for her daughter's five cavities."

This was not new. It blew my mind how often my mother got the blame for the state of other people's children's teeth. She saw them once every six months. What did they think she was doing, drilling little holes into their teeth to make sure cavities formed later?

"Ouch."

"Yeah, and Dr. Joshi had a fainter, so we had the paramedics in again. Last patient of the day, of course."

"Diabetic?" I asked. It had happened before.

She smiled at me. "This is why you're my favorite child. You listen to my stories and remember them."

"I'm your only child."

"Still counts. How about you?" she asked, eyeing my lip. "How did you feel today? Did you eat?"

I crossed my heart. And my stomach rumbled, loud. Traitor.

She laughed. "I'm sensing a growth spurt."

"Go have your shower. I'll go make dinner happen faster."

She waved and was off down the hallway.

"Okay," I said, regarding my bedroom door. "Pay attention."

I stepped through my bedroom door into the hall, as slow as I could, and hyper-aware. I felt that...*something*. Like a *tug*, or a pull that seemed to hook into the center of my chest behind my ribs. It held on to me for a second, and I wondered where I'd go if I let the tug pull on me.

No. Nope. Nada. Cole, stay put. Now was not the time. Parents. Dinner.

I pushed past it, and there was sort of a *snap* sensation as it let go.

I was in the hallway. Successfully.

Check me out. I had just triumphed over the modern door.

I raised my fist a second time, then went to find my dad.

❖

You feeling better? my dad signed between slicing up green peppers. He was standing at the island. It looked like a stir-fry was in the making. Simple, quick, but when my dad cooked, it was always amazing. He'd tried to teach me some of the basics, but the way he cooked—he just threw stuff together and it was always incredible—was for people who had a natural talent for cooking, and I was not a natural. Following recipes was right up my alley. You followed the instructions and ended up with edible food. I could do that. I didn't ignore what he suggested when he told me I could do something different than what the recipes said. I just never did if I was cooking something myself.

Today? Up and down, I signed in reply. Truth by omission was the new black. *Today, Mom also feels up and down! Sooner Mom eats, sooner Mom can crash.*

He smiled and pointed at the mushrooms. I brought them to the island and started slicing them up opposite my dad.

Today down what? he asked before starting another pepper.

"This." I pointed to my lip. "I was the hot topic of the day."

Tell them you in bar fight?

I laughed. "That's what Grayson suggested." I exaggerated my expression of amusement.

My dad paused. *Don't-know how I feel about that.* He screwed up his face comically. Grayson's ability to alienate the people around him didn't limit itself to kids my age, though I wasn't sure if he'd ever said something directly to my dad, or if my dad was just reacting to what he'd heard about Grayson from me. Grayson didn't come over much, and my dad was somewhat aware of the fallout from last year's disaster between Grayson and Alec. And of the Rainbow Club, only Alec really dropped by. Dad was firmly Team Alec.

Well, because many people saw me faint, it doesn't matter.

He nodded, picked the knife back up, and set to chopping again.

Once I was done with the mushrooms and he'd finished his second pepper, he stopped again.

Today up what?

Right. I'd told him there was good stuff today, too. I took the mushrooms over to the wok, where chicken was already sizzling, and poured them in, stirring it up and flipping the little chunks of chicken. They were turning white as they cooked.

When I turned back, he was still waiting for me. Luckily, my delaying had given me time to find the right, totally-not-a-lie words.

"I think I got a handle on some stuff that was worrying me," I said, remembering my return from our old house to my bedroom. I fought hard to keep eye contact with him. See? Totally the truth. Just maybe a bit light on the honesty.

He did that laser-eye dad thing again, like he was reading way more than my signs.

If you need to talk, he signed, then tapped the center of his chest. *I know a genius.*

"Me too," I said. "But she's in the shower."

He put a hand to his heart like I'd stabbed him, but the smile gave him away.

God, I was lucky. He was a ham and didn't know when to quit, but I couldn't have asked for a better freaking dad.

We worked across the island for a little while, my dad making the sauce and me setting up the rice steamer. All the veggies went in with the chicken and then Dad covered it with a sauce he'd magically assembled from his own head involving soy sauce and tomatoes and other stuff from the spice rack and various cans and some sort of alchemy.

"Smells good." My mother came into the kitchen. Her hair was still damp but pulled back in a ponytail, and she had on one of Dad's university T-shirts and a pair of khaki shorts.

Dad tapped his lips, and my mother leaned in for a kiss. They smiled at each other, and I stared down at the rice steamer because when they looked at each other like that, I could never decide if it was the most awesome thing in the world or if it was really, really gross.

Once they were done being gross awesome parents in love, my dad leaned over and checked the timer.

Five minutes, he signed.

I'll set table. Watching them move around each other while she gathered cutlery and paper napkins was like watching them dance. They touched each other in passing, little touches that weren't necessary but made my mom smile and my dad wink. It was adorable.

And gross.

Really, it was a wonder I'd ever made it out of therapy. Didn't they know their kid was watching?

The timer flashed, and Dad started serving onto the three plates my mother had left for him.

My stomach growled again.

Man, I was hungry.

I wondered how many calories it took to teleport.

To-Do

- ■ Bring home calculus textbook
- ☐ Exam prep: calculus, biology
- ☐ Exam prep: English (reread?)
- ☐ Exam prep: French (practice exam!)
- ☐ Movie night with Alec this w/e?
- ■ Make lunch for Tuesday, slacker
- ■ "What happened?" joke
- ☐ Laundry
- ☐ Slap Malik King
- ☐ Doors? DOORS! Definitely Doors.
- ☐ Alec at RC on Thursday
- ☐ Hungry?

EIGHT

Wednesday morning, I stumbled out of my bedroom a bit late after one too many hits of snooze and ended up standing on the front step outside the door in my pajama bottoms.

Scrambling back in through the front door—if there was a God, no one saw that—I found myself staring right at my dad, who stood just inside the kitchen, decidedly groggy. He was turning on the coffee machine. When he saw me coming in from outside, he frowned at me.

Everything okay?

Need to brush teeth, I signed, dodging past him to get to the stairs before he could ask any questions about why I'd been in the front yard in my bare feet and pajamas if I needed to brush my teeth. This time, when I went through the door to the bathroom, I remembered to pay attention. The little tug-then-snap sensation happened again, but I made it to the sink.

This teleporting thing wasn't going away. As far as plans went, "ignore it" was officially a spectacular failure and off the table. Time to face facts.

"Hi, my name is Cole, and I have a teleporting problem," I said, staring at myself in the mirror.

"Hi Cole," I replied, in a deeper voice. "Your lip looks less gross today. Also, you realize you're talking to yourself, right?"

I brushed my teeth, spat, rinsed, and had a shower. By the time I dried off, I'd made a decision. This was no different than self-defense classes or calculus. Neither of those things had come naturally. I'd had to work at them, so I needed to practice. Standing in the middle of the bathroom, I opened the door and looked across the hallway to my bedroom. The door was still open from when I'd accidentally ended up outside.

I took a step, staring at my bedroom and willing myself to skip the hallway and just be there.

It didn't work. I was in the hallway. Annoyed, I went to my bedroom door and paused. I was wearing a towel. Now was not the time to teleport somewhere else.

"Just going to my room to get dressed," I muttered to myself.

I crossed the threshold. Another tug-and-snap. But I was in my room.

How in the world was I going to practice this?

"Cole!" my mother yelled from downstairs. "Ten minutes!"

I glanced at the clock. Crap. I dressed quickly, grabbed my backpack, and made it through my bedroom door without incident again. I needed to grab some toast and then run for the bus, or I'd have to walk it and might end up late.

❖

"Hey, Cole?"

Malik King was standing over me. I'd eaten my lunch and was just waiting out the clock with cowardice so I wouldn't bump into Grayson or the rest of the club.

Given that I was sitting with my back against one of the trees along the track field, I didn't look up so much as I looked *way* up. Boy was tall.

"Yeah?" I said. It came out of my throat a bit wary, which wasn't exactly polite. Cute or not, I wasn't sure how I felt about Malik having come by the Rainbow Club to drop his little bomb yesterday.

He bit his lip. Okay, so he wasn't just cute. He was kind of hot. Okay, he was really hot. Oh, let's be clear: the boy was on fire. How in the world he could make a plain red T-shirt do all the things it was doing for him I'd never know, but now I felt bad about my less-than-warm greeting.

"Sorry," we both said at the same time.

"What?" we both said a beat later.

He held up a hand. I closed my mouth.

"Can I sit?" he said.

I nodded. Okay. Malik wanted to sit with me. That was…what *was* that?

He sat. He was playing with an orange, not peeling it, just rolling it around in his hands.

"I thought you would have told them," he said. "About the locker. I'm really sorry."

He was staring at his orange like looking at me would be a bad idea. I felt bad. From his point of view, it really did look like something I should have brought up, right? If I'd really been shoved into a locker, I damn well would have told the rest of the Rainbow Club. There's no way I'd put up with that crap.

"It's okay," I said.

He looked at me. He was doing that eyebrow thing again. It was a really, really good look for him.

"Really," I said.

"How's your lip?"

I fought the urge to cover my mouth with my hand. "It's okay."

"I guess I left too soon, eh?"

"Low blood sugar isn't sweet."

He smiled and did this little half-chuckle.

Oh my God. Did I just successfully tell a joke to a cute boy?

"Your friends…" Malik said, and then he stopped. He was back to staring at his orange.

"My friends?"

"They're not mad at you, right? I mean, it really sucks when your friends are mad at you."

Huh. I looked at him. Was it just me or was there more going on here? The way he fiddled with the orange, the way he wasn't looking at me. Body language. I wasn't my dad, but…

What reason would your friends ever have to be mad at you? I thought. Goose pimples broke out across my arms.

"What?" he said.

I blinked. "Sorry, uh…" I swallowed. "I don't think so. I mean, they might be after we talk, but they're not mad right now. I'm maybe avoiding them in the meanwhile."

"Why would they be mad after you talk to them?"

"I'm officially going to tell them I don't want to do anything about the whole locker thing."

"Ah." He finally started to peel the orange. "I bet they'll be okay. They seem cool."

I smiled. "They are. But I'm still rewarding myself with Meeples after."

Malik glanced at me. "That board game place?"

"It's sort of the best place ever."

"Haven't been," he said.

"This is my surprised face," I said, though I tried not to sound too mean about it. "It's more my crowd than yours." When he raised his eyebrow—he needed to do that less often if I was going to manage to remember how to speak in coherent sentences—I added, "That's not a dig. It's an observation. I am at one with my geekness. Have you ever seen me throw a sportsball? I don't sportsball well."

"Sportsball?" He laughed when he said it, though.

"I rest my case."

"Hey, King, you slumming? Community outreach with Colenap doesn't count for your volunteer hours, y'know."

We both turned to see Austin walking by with his two usual accessories, Billy and Ethan.

"Fuck off, Austin," Malik said in this cool, included way. He threw some of his orange peel at him, too. Austin laughed, dodging it, then kept moving. He was gone a second later.

I stared at the ground. What was that I'd just been saying about our respective crowds? Of all the times for a drive-by Colenapping.

"Can I ask you something?" Malik said.

And there it was. I sighed. I hated this question.

"I don't remember," I said. "Like, anything."

He frowned at me.

"I was four years old, and as far as I know, she didn't do anything to me. I mean, yeah. She apparently snatched me, locked me up in her backyard, and kept me for the afternoon, but even the doctors checked me out and couldn't find anything worse than a cat scratch. She was a crazy old cat lady, not a pedophile. No, I don't have nightmares. Yes, I still like cats. Yes, my parents barely let me out of their sight. Any other questions?"

Malik was staring at me now, his eyes wide. I realized I'd raised my voice.

"Sorry," I said. "It's…I just really hate that name. Colenap. It's… stupid, but…whatever."

"That's not what…" Malik cleared his throat. "That wasn't what I meant."

"Oh." Oh man. Maybe I could have a heart attack and die right now? That might be good.

"Austin's an asshole," Malik said.

"Yes."

He finished peeling his orange and pulled off a section. I tried not to stare while he ate it. I mostly failed. He caught me looking and did the eyebrow thing again. Paralyzing.

"So, what was the question?" I said.

"Never mind." He shook his head. "It's okay. I just wanted to apologize for the other day." He popped another slice of the orange into his mouth.

He was eating his orange pretty quickly now, like it was the top of his to-do list, and he was going to check it off ASAP. I was pretty sure I'd just messed something up.

"Anyway," he said, wiping his hands on his jeans as the last piece disappeared. "I'll see you around."

"Okay," I said, mystified.

He rose and walked off.

"It's really okay," I said, a little louder than maybe I needed to. But he turned and smiled and waved before he went back toward the school.

My phone buzzed.

Are you hiding again? It was Grayson.

I'll have you know I was hanging out with Malik King, thankyouveverymuch. I hit Send.

BS. You're hiding by the trees, aren't you?

I smiled. *Busted*, I sent.

Be there in five.

I leaned back against the tree. I should probably enjoy the last five minutes of quiet I was about to have of my lunch break. I looked up.

The same substitute teacher from Tuesday was back, staring at me from the same spot on the field. I shuddered and looked back at my phone. I wondered if people would find bodies buried in the guy's basement someday. I couldn't put a finger on why he set off my rando-freak alert, but I didn't much care. Even a substitute teacher should know better than to just stand there in a field watching kids eat their lunch, right?

When Grayson showed up, I looked again.

Bearded creepy guy was gone.

Huzzah.

I grabbed my bullet journal while Grayson talked at me about a song I hadn't heard, and it reminded me I needed to make a plan for biology. That was definitely what I'd do tonight. Then I turned to a new page and started a new list. This morning, I'd been standing at my front door in nothing but my pajama bottoms.

After biology?

It was time to get serious about being a freak of nature.

To-Do

- ■ Bring home calculus textbook
- ■ Exam prep: calculus, biology
- ☐ Exam prep: English (reread?)
- ☐ Exam prep: French (practice exam!)
- ☐ Movie night with Alec this w/e?
- ■ Make lunch for Tuesday, slacker
- ■ "What happened?" joke
- ■ Laundry
- ☐ Slap Malik King
- ☐ ~~Doors? DOORS! Definitely Doors.~~
- ☐ Alec at RC on Thursday
- ☐ ~~Hungry?~~
- ☐ Calculus: practice derivatives
- ☐ Biology: review biochem and metabolic processes

Cole the Teenage Freak

- ☐ Concentrate at doors. All the doors. Every time.
- ☐ Locked doors. One way?
- ☐ Blood sugar? Hungry?
- ☐ CARRY YOUR PHONE.

NINE

W hen Alec showed up at the club meeting with me, it got a little quiet. The tugging sensation as I passed through the door had been pretty intense, and I half stumbled getting through, like maybe I just barely escaped another trip. Alec put a hand on my back, and the little snap sensation let me go.

That had been close. God, what if I'd teleported away right then and there?

On the other hand, I could have skipped the whole club meeting if I had. And I bet vanishing in front of them would make them drop the locker thing real quick. I smiled at the thought while I took my seat in the circle of chairs, and Alec sat beside me. Grayson stared at him across the circle. You could have cut the tension in the room with a knife.

Why had I thought this was a good idea again?

Alec ignored Grayson and gave me a little smile.

Oh. Right. Backup.

"Good to see you," Rhonda said. She was talking to Alec. He bobbed his head in her direction.

Nat went through the usual welcome and read over the last meeting's notes. The complete lack of mention of my locker revelation sort of hung there when they were done. "The only thing on our plate is going to be planning our year-end party, unless anyone else wants to bring something forward," they said, putting the notepad down.

"About that," I said. All eyes were on me. I'd rehearsed this. That was how I did public speaking. That was how my whole "Born to Those Who Aren't Like You" speech had done so well. I wasn't good at the spontaneous making of words. I was good at practice. "I know it's maybe not what any of you were hoping for, but I don't want to do or say anything about the whole locker thing. There's nothing I can say, and I hope you all trust me enough to know I wouldn't lie about that. There's no one I can point a finger at and say, 'You. You did this.'"

Well, y'know, without a mirror.

I watched their faces. Grayson was scowling, but he didn't say anything, a fact I attributed to Alec staring him down. Nat was trying for blank, but they looked sad, which sort of felt like a gut punch. Lindsey was holding Rhonda's hand, and Rhonda nodded at me.

"If—" Grayson started. Alec shifted in his seat beside me.

Grayson held up his hand. "I wasn't going to argue. I was just going to say if you change your mind, we've got your back. You do what you gotta do to be happy."

Whoa. For Grayson, that was…almost deep. Alec leaned back in his chair, no doubt just as surprised as I was.

"Okay," Nat said, when no one else spoke up. "I reached out to the other GSAs, and they're all pretty sure they're down with joining us for a party, including Central."

We batted around a few more ideas, but it was obvious we'd all petered out. Nat called it a meeting.

"Okay," I said. "Anyone want to go to Meeples?" I did my best puppy eyes. "Just for an hour, even? I do need to study tonight, too." I had a date with both biology and calculus.

"Catan?" Lindsey said. She grinned at me. An exceptional counteroffer on her part, as she almost always won Settlers of Catan, but it meant she was in if I was willing to suffer another crippling blow to my board game ego.

Happily, I was.

"Deal," I said. "Rhonda?" I aimed my eyes her way, full-puppy.

"Sure," Rhonda said, like I knew she would. Rhonda didn't care that Lindsey always won, which was probably one of the things that made their relationship so amazing.

"You guys have fun," Alec said, heading off the invitation.

"But *lattes*," I said. "Mocha lattes with almond shots. And date squares. And lemon bars."

He wavered. I had him, and I knew it. I would feel bad about it, but I was too busy relishing the triumph. I wanted all my favorite people around me. And maybe even Grayson, too.

"Grayson? Nat?" Lindsey asked. "There's a six-player expansion."

"You had me at lemon bars," Grayson said.

"I'm down for caffeine," Nat said. "But I'll just watch. Candice is awesome, and we should support our local allies."

I had a moment of brilliance. "Meeples!" I said.

Everyone looked at me.

"Yes," Grayson said. "We know. We're all coming to your geek nest."

"No," I said. "We could throw the end-of-the-year party at Meeples. I'm sure Candice would let us, and we could support her with what money we could gather. She sponsored us for Pride, remember? And like Malik said, she's got great food and stuff for the people who don't want to play games. But the games *are* a great way to mingle, too, right? I mean, we had that whole 'wall of people' problem last year with no one really dancing for half the night. Games would get people sitting together and talking." I saw Lindsey frowning, and thought quickly. "Not *instead* of dancing, though. I'm sure she'd let us clear a small spot for dancing if we wanted to."

"And it's not licensed," Nat said. "So it wouldn't mean any extra work."

"You think the other groups would come from the city?" Grayson said. "To play *board games*?"

"Well," I said, deflating a little. "It's *different*. Why not? We can ask, right?" I wasn't going to let Grayson stop me from getting excited. "I mean, there's no harm in asking."

Alec threw his arm around my neck. "You're such a geek."

"Proud of it," I said. "Seriously, though. What do you guys think?"

Rhonda was smiling, and even Lindsey looked amenable. If I could get her to consider it, I knew we were set. She was the social heart of our group.

"It could be cool," she said.

"At the least, I can ask Candice if she'd be willing and then float it to the other GSAs," Nat said.

"I love all of you so much right now," I said.

Alec tugged me in and kissed the top of my head. "C'mon," he said. "I'll drive."

❖

"I take it it went okay?"

I'd gone to the counter to put in our order—heavy on the lemon bars—and was second in line when the last voice I expected in the world spoke up right behind me. I turned.

Malik King. At Meeples.

"Turns out you were right. They're good people," I said.

He smiled. "I'm glad." He looked honestly relieved, too, like he'd been worried.

"You really didn't do anything wrong," I said.

He did a sort of half-shrug. "I should have asked you first, instead of just going to your meeting."

"Well," I said, which was all I could think to say since I agreed with him. Mentally, I decided I didn't need to fight him anymore, which was good because he could totally take me. "It worked out."

The guy in front of me left with his coffee, and I stepped up. I rattled off my large order, and Candice rang me through. I paid up and then stepped to the side to wait for her to make all the various lattes and teas and plate all the wedges of sugar and lemon.

"I take it the lemon bars are good?" Malik said.

"They're amazing, though I also love the date squares."

"I get them from the same baker as Bittersweets," Candice said, name-dropping the awesome smaller chain of fair-sourced coffee shops in Ottawa.

"Now I know what I'll order," Malik said.

"You should join us," I said. "We're playing Settlers of Catan."

He raised an eyebrow. "I don't know. Is there room for a sportsballer? I mean, this isn't where *my* crowd goes, right?"

I winced. "So, that sounds terrible when you say it like that. Which is how I said it. Which means it was terrible when I said it."

"Is it easy to learn?" he asked. "I don't want to hold *your* crowd back."

"See, now you're making me feel even worse. Seriously. Come join us," I said. Candice already had the bars on the plates. I picked them up, balancing them with a precarious arrangement of fingers and thumbs.

"I'll be right there," he said.

I carried the plates over. Lindsey was still setting up the board, building one of the larger maps.

"Do we have room for Malik to join us?" I said.

"He can totally have my spot," Alec said.

"It can handle six," Lindsey said. "If Nat still doesn't want to play, there's room."

"I'm good," Nat said, already biting into their lemon bar.

Candice called out the first two lattes, and I went back to the bar to get them.

"Good news," I said to Malik. "You're in."

I got another raised eyebrow. I was starting to realize his raised eyebrow thing came in different kinds. This one was sort of playful. Also, I was starting to enjoy them a little too much.

To no one's surprise, Lindsey won. But unless I was really mistaken or Malik was a phenomenal actor, he looked like he was having fun, and he scored the largest army, which put him in second place.

"Another round?" Lindsey asked, flashing her butter-wouldn't-melt smile.

"I have to get home," I said. "Biology."

"Me too," Nat said.

"They always leave first. They're *responsible*," Grayson said, leaning over to Malik. "You in?" To my surprise, he'd been pretty low-key for the game. He'd even made a few trades with Malik that weren't entirely in his own favor. I wasn't sure what was up with Grayson, but I liked it. He hadn't even made a single snide comment to Alec the entire game. That had to be a record. Even better, it meant I didn't have to smack him down in front of Malik.

"I should head out, too," Malik said.

Grayson shook his head. "Kids today. Am I enough for you?" he asked Lindsey.

She put a hand over her heart. "You're the only man I'll ever need."

We all laughed, even Malik.

"You need a ride?" Alec asked me.

"Aw, kisses. But I think I'll walk," I said. It was nice out.

"You good Saturday night for a movie night?" Alec said.

"All the yes." I picked up my bag and slung it over my shoulder. "Whose turn to pick?"

"Mine," Alec said.

That meant I was in for something sweet and romantic, most likely. You wouldn't know it to look at the lug, but Alec was all about the feels.

"Which way are you headed?" Malik asked.

"Past the locks."

"Do you mind if I join you?"

"Of course," I said. "I mean yes. I mean, *no*, I don't mind." I swallowed and snapped my mouth shut before it could do any more damage. Thank God Grayson had been talking to Lindsey and Rhonda, or I'd never have lived that one down. As it was, Alec had a massive grin on his face, so I knew I'd hear about my verbal vomit later.

"Cool," he said, grabbing his bag.

When he'd turned his back and was heading for the door, Grayson waved to get my attention. I looked at him.

He pointed at Malik's back, then at me, then lifted both hands. It wasn't ASL, but the meaning was pretty clear.

Dude, you and Malik? What's up with that?

"No idea," I mouthed, and I left them at the table.

To-Do

- ■ Bring home calculus textbook
- ■ Exam prep: calculus, biology
- ☐ Exam prep: English (reread?)
- ☐ Exam prep: French (practice exam!)
- ☐ Movie night with Alec this w/e?
- ■ Make lunch for Tuesday, slacker
- ■ "What happened?" joke
- ■ Laundry
- ☐ ~~Slap Malik King~~
- ☐ ~~Doors? DOORS! Definitely Doors.~~
- ■ Alec at RC on Thursday
- ☐ ~~Hungry?~~
- ☐ Calculus: practice derivatives
- ☐ Biology: review biochem and metabolic processes

Cole the Teenage Freak

- ☐ Concentrate at doors. All the doors. Every time.
- ☐ Locked doors. One way?
- ☐ Blood sugar? Hungry?
- ☐ CARRY YOUR PHONE.

TEN

M alik had ridden his bike, but he walked it beside me.
"So what did you think of Meeples?" I said.

"Great lemon bars," he said.

"Wait until you try the date squares."

"And the game was fun."

I smiled. "I'm so glad. Meeples is in my top five, so if you'd hated it, I'm not sure I'd be allowed to speak with you ever again."

"Wow. That sounds harsh."

"Top fives are important."

"You have five favorite stores?" Malik said. "I don't think I could come up with five." He frowned, considering. "Yeah, maybe three?"

"Not stores," I said. "Just places. Happy places. It's a list, sort of the other half of the five places I want to go list."

"Oh," Malik said. "What's number one?"

"This cabin in Sooke," I said, without pausing to think.

"Sooke?"

"It's in B.C. I went there on vacation once with my parents. It's the middle of nowhere, but it was really pretty. I got to draw a lot and I got to see the ocean."

"And Meeples is on the same list?" He sounded dubious.

"Well, it's a list of places I've been, and between you and me, I haven't been many places. Like, number two is a Deaf camp."

That gave him pause. "Really?"

I smiled. "When I was a kid, my folks weren't good with me being out of sight, because…" I faltered, and he gave me a nod to show he got it. *Colenap.* Right. Moving on. "Anyway, there's this camp where kids who are Deaf or hard of hearing or who have Deaf or hard of hearing parents can go. That was the first time they really let me go somewhere without them, y'know? And it was pretty amazing. Like, there's a whole bunch of stuff that comes with having my dad, and all those other kids? They got it. Everyone could sign, everyone understood deafie humor..." I looked at him, realizing I'd been blabbering again, but he didn't look at me like I was speaking in tongues.

"I get it," he said.

The surprise must have shown on my face, because he did the eyebrow thing again. "Do you have any idea how many times I've been asked where I'm from?"

"Ah," I said. There were maybe a dozen kids in our high school who weren't white.

"Meeples is third, then?"

"Meeples is fifth," I admitted. "Three is this diner in Ottawa, and four is the canal in winter. What about you?"

"I don't have a list," he said. "But I got to see a game at the SkyDome once, and that was amazing."

"I've heard of that place," I said. "They play sportsball there."

He smiled again.

"So would that be number one?"

"You're really into lists, aren't you?" he said.

"Maybe you've noticed I'm a bit of a geek," I said.

His lips twitched. "Maybe."

"Well, I love lists. To-do lists, color coding, I am at one with the way of the bullet journal."

"That sounds lethal."

"It's *so* not. It's probably the least cool thing you can do with a notebook, but I love it." I shrugged. I owned my nerd side. "I make lists in it of places I've been or places I want to go, things that give me hope, books I want to read...y'know. Lists."

We waited for the lights to change.

"So, where do you want to go?" he asked once the light changed. "One through five."

"Easy. Jasper, because despite my sportsball failings, I'm not entirely unskilled on a pair of skis; Iceland, I totally want to see the Northern Lights; the Louvre—because duh; Stonewall, because I want to see the history; and the Grand Canyon—also duh."

He blinked. "Okay, you are really organized." He paused. "Why is the Louvre a duh?"

"I want to draw some of my favorite pieces of art. And FYI, you're totally allowed to get on your bike and leave me here if you want," I said. "I'm told hanging out with me doesn't count for your volunteer hours."

He snorted. "Austin is an asshole. And I bet he doesn't even know where the Louvre is."

I smiled. Okay, that was a super-nice thing to say. "Your turn. Five places you'd like to see." He squirmed, so I said, "No pressure."

He took a few seconds, and we crossed the street before he replied again.

"Okay," he said. "I've had no time to really think about this, so no saying any of these are lame."

"Dude," I said. "I want to go to the *Louvre*."

"Fair enough. Okay. Vimy for sure. Oh, the Eye, in London. Café du Monde, Chicago, and…New York. I'm not sure on the order there, but definitely those five. At least, right this second."

"Café du Monde?" I said. I didn't know it. Also, Vimy? I was expecting five sports arenas. Color me impressed.

"It's in New Orleans," Malik said. "They serve beignets. They're donuts with powdered sugar."

I smiled. "Donuts? I think we have those here."

He shook his head. "Not to hear my mom tell it."

"She goes to New Orleans a lot?"

"Yeah, and Chicago and New York," he said. "Writing conventions."

"Your mom's a writer?" I may have sounded really enthused, but come on. She wrote books? That was *really* cool.

He nodded. "She writes mystery novels. Dita Wallace. That's her maiden name. She won an Edgar last year."

I shook my head. "I don't know what that means, but it sounds cool."

"It's a big mystery award thing," he said. "She's sort of awesome. Except when you try to watch Netflix. Then she's all, 'Oh, it was the ex-wife' thirty seconds into the show, and she gets mad when they do DNA testing in a couple of hours and stuff. She's a walking spoiler."

I laughed. We were at my street. I paused and pointed. "I'm this way."

Malik bit his lip. Then he took a deep breath and said, "How did you know?"

I frowned, replaying the conversation. Beignets, Netflix, spoilers… "How did I know what?"

He stared at me. It took me *way* longer than it should have to click.

"Oh," I said. Because *oh. Oh wow.*

He blew out a little breath. I noticed he had a death grip on his bike.

"Um," I said. I tried to remember everything Nat had always said about being a supportive role-model and what to say and how to listen and...I drew a complete and utter blank. Instead, all I was thinking was *Malik King? Holy shit!*

I needed to answer him.

"Honestly? I just didn't feel the way everyone else did. Like, when the other guys started talking about girls, I was already friends with the girls, but way more interested in how the girls were talking about the guys, if that makes sense. It was sort of obvious to me after that."

He nodded, but now he wasn't looking at me. I felt like I was doing this wrong. Some of what Nat always talked about seeped back into my brain, finally.

"Malik," I said. "Thank you for asking me. And just so you know? You can trust me. You can ask me anything, and I promise you I won't say anything to anyone, okay?"

He let out another shaky breath. "Thanks." He swallowed. "I like girls." He sort of blurted it out. In fact, he sounded almost angry about it, like it made things harder or something. "I do. I'm not...like...faking or anything."

"That's allowed," I said. He frowned at me. "I didn't mean faking, I meant being into girls. You can be into girls *and* boys. It's allowed. Rhonda's bi. And Nat is pan."

"Pan?" he said. He wasn't quite looking at me, though he was looking more or less in my direction.

"Pansexual," I said. "They're into people of any gender. So, if they like someone, they like someone."

"How's that different from bi?"

"Oh, well, it's..." I blinked. "I honestly don't know. I'm not sure there is a difference. At least, I think it's pretty much the same. Or, I think that's what Nat says, but between you and me, they're so far ahead of me I sometimes just nod and agree and promise myself I'll Google stuff later." I wondered if I was helping. I didn't feel like I was helping.

Malik nodded. He'd barely moved. His shoulders were ramrod straight, and the grip on his bike looked almost painful to me.

"Malik, are you okay?"

"I never...said that before."

Another click. "Oh my God, was this what you wanted to ask me on the field?"

"Yeah." His neck darkened.

And I'd ranted at him about *Colenap*. Ugh! "I'm so sorry. I'm such an idiot."

He laughed. And though it was a shaky laugh, the sound was really welcome. "It's fine. Really."

"And that's why you came to Meeples?"

He nodded.

We stood there a few seconds longer.

It was getting awkward. I could tell he wanted to go.

"You can text me or message me or whatever," I said. "Any time. I mean it. I know this can be hard."

"Okay." He finally let go of his bike and pulled out his phone. His hand was shaking, and we both pretended not to notice while I gave him my number. After that, he *maybe* looked a little more relaxed, but he *definitely* seemed ready to go.

"Thanks," he said.

"Thanks for coming to Meeples," I said.

He nodded, then he got on his bike and was gone. Fast. Like, maybe if he pedaled hard enough, he'd forget what we just talked about. Poor guy. I remembered my own first terrifying moment of telling someone—Alec, though that had turned out to be the best thing ever. I hoped I'd done a good job, but I was pretty sure I fell short of someone hugging me and letting me cry.

All the stuff Nat had drilled into us about being supportive was coming back now. I walked the last of the way home replaying everything I said, didn't say, and probably should have said. I felt dumb. I mean, I'd told myself a thousand times I'd be there for anyone who wanted to come out to me. But I'd never imagined it would be someone like Malik King.

Okay, maybe that was untrue. At one point or another, I'd imagined all the guys I found attractive telling me they were gay. Usually, they were also asking me to go the prom and begging forgiveness for ignoring me all the time. I had whole speeches ready for the moment someone asked me to prom. It turned out I hadn't needed any of them. A bunch of us just went as friends, but it was always good to be prepared.

I blew out a breath and went home. I got through the front door without any trouble and went to my room after a quick hello to my dad.

The plan was to spend quality time studying. Instead, I went online to find the differences between bisexual and pansexual. It turned out there was no clear answer, but wow did people have opinions and really angry Tumblr wars about it. Then I found myself looking at pictures of New Orleans and checking out Café du Monde. I added it to my bullet journal on my list of places I'd like to visit someday. I put a little star beside it and did a few quick strokes with my pencil of the cool fence that surrounded the café in the picture.

When my mom got home, I went down to help her with dinner. Maybe I'd crack my biology textbook after we ate.

Yeah, right.

To-Do

- ■ Bring home calculus textbook
- ■ Exam prep: calculus, biology
- ☐ Exam prep: English (reread?)
- ☐ Exam prep: French (practice exam!)
- ☐ Movie night with Alec this w/e?
- ■ Make lunch for Tuesday, slacker
- ■ "What happened?" joke
- ■ Laundry
- ☐ ~~Slap Malik King~~
- ☐ ~~Doors? DOORS! Definitely Doors.~~
- ■ Alec at RC on Thursday
- ☐ ~~Hungry?~~
- ☐ Calculus: practice derivatives
- ☐ Biology: review biochem and metabolic processes
- ☐ Bi/Pan?
- ☐ Check in with Sportsball Star

Cole the Teenage Freak

- ■ ~~Concentrate at doors. All the doors. Every time.~~ You got this!
- ☐ Locked doors. One way?
- ☐ Blood sugar? Hungry?
- ☐ CARRY YOUR PHONE.

Eleven

"W ho are you looking for?"

It shouldn't have been a surprise Rhonda caught me out. She was like that. She watched. It was raining, so most of the student body was back inside for lunch, and most of the Rainbow Club were at our usual table in the cafeteria. I'd been trying—unsuccessfully, I guess—to subtly check around to see if I could spot Malik anywhere. He hadn't made eye contact with me in homeroom, and other than that, I'd not seen him at all. I could see his friends at one of the tables, but not him. I was beginning to think I'd royally screwed up what I was supposed to do and was wondering if I had a way to fix it.

Thing was, he'd sent no texts, so I didn't know if that was a sign I should back off, or I should worry, or...?

"Cole?" Rhonda said.

"Sorry," I said. "It's nothing. I'm probably overthinking something."

"You?" Grayson said from across the table. "*No.*" He put a hand on his heart. Or at least, where his heart would be if he had one.

"Your lip looks better," Lindsey said.

I smiled. "Thanks."

"Seriously, though, who are you looking for?" Grayson said.

"No one," I said, putting Malik firmly out of mind. Right. Like that would last. I turned back to Rhonda. "Hey, what's the difference between bi and pan?"

She raised an eyebrow. I'd never noticed she could do that before. Huh. Maybe it was a bisexual thing.

"It's just...I'm not clear on it," I said. "I'd ask Nat but half the time I don't understand the answers when they give them to me."

Rhonda gave me a rare little smile for that. "Short answer? It depends. People say bi or pan to mean different things. Some think one sounds too binary, some think the other is false advertising, it's…" She paused, as though she were aware she was using up what amounted to three months' worth of her usual spoken words to me in one go. "Complicated." She looked at Lindsey and smiled. "For me? It means when I looked at her, I knew I was done for."

Lindsey put a hand over her heart, which I was pretty sure had just grown a few sizes. Grayson stole one of her fries during the moment. Opportunist.

"Got it," I said. Well, actually I got *nothing*, but at least now I knew even my bisexual friend didn't have a clue. I felt a little less like I'd failed Malik when he'd asked.

And that prompted another scan of the cafeteria. Was he avoiding everyone or just me?

"You're doing it again," Grayson said.

"Leave him alone," Lindsey said.

"Yes, Mom."

"Ugh. I am *so* not a mom."

"Okay, Mom."

"I will hurt you."

I watched the two nudge and bump each other for a few seconds, checked my phone—nothing—and then opened my bullet journal and put a little question mark beside my reminder to check in with Malik. Then I started working on a quick scribble-sketch of Lindsey and Grayson sitting beside each other.

"Are you drawing me?" Grayson said.

"No."

"Liar."

"I'm drawing you *both*. I want to remember you fondly from far, far away."

"He's lying again," Lindsey said. "He's only going to remember *me* fondly."

I grinned over my journal while Grayson nudged Lindsey's shoulder.

"I will be remembered fondly," Grayson said, in a haughty, put-upon voice. "I've come to the realization I'm worth love."

All my arm hair stood on end, and I shivered.

"You okay?" Rhonda said.

"Anyone ever tell you you're creepy perceptive?" I said. I swear, between Rhonda and my dad, it was a wonder I could breathe without someone pointing it out.

"Thank you!" Lindsey said.

Rhonda just looked at me.

"It's nothing," I said. Because I wasn't sure *what* it was. Just... something. Coincidence, I guess, that I'd been thinking that about Grayson just the other day. *Worth loving.* I looked around again, but before Grayson could razz me about it, I saw Alec coming out of the lineup with a tray, and I waved at him. He came over.

"*Do you mind* if I join you?" he said, grinning at me.

Oh, that was how it was gonna be, was it?

"Sure, sit," Rhonda said. Happily, neither she nor Grayson had been paying attention enough to hear my verbal vomit with Malik at Meeples yesterday.

I checked for Malik again while Alec sat with us. Nothing.

"Hey," Alec said, nodding to the others. Lindsey and Grayson nodded back.

I eyed Grayson warily, but...nothing. Grayson seemed to be content to continue bugging Lindsey in his low-key way. Well, low-key for him.

"Crap," Alec said.

I looked at him. He pointed to his tray, where he had a plate of spaghetti and some garlic bread, and nothing else.

"Gonna eat that with your hands?" I said.

"Apparently." He stared at the tray, like maybe some cutlery would just appear by magic.

"I'm gonna go buy a drink," I said, rising. "I can grab you a fork." The line had finally gotten short enough that it wasn't sticking out through the in door.

"*Do you mind?*" Alec said, ripping off a piece of his garlic bread and grinning at me.

I narrowed my eyes but decided I'd be the bigger person and get him a fork anyway. I really did need a drink. I'd intended to bring a can of root beer from home, but the usual morning rush at Casa Tozer had included my dad this morning, so I had to make my own and I'd forgotten to grab anything to drink. They didn't have root beer at the school, but at least I could get a Coke or something, and—

Tug-snap. Poof.

I was in my kitchen.

"Oh come *on*." I'd pushed through the stupid flappy-door at the cafeteria without thinking about it and now here I was, at home, and this was getting so *old*. I swore, loud.

Then I froze. Was my father home? I took a deep breath and listened. I didn't hear anything. Oh, right. Of course he wasn't home. Duh. He'd had an appointment out of town for an in-person interpreting assignment, which had been part of how I'd gotten to school without my root beer.

I rolled my shoulders and relaxed. Okay. So I'd slipped up. At least it was my own kitchen. I shrugged and went to the fridge. If I'd accidentally teleported home, I'd grab myself a root beer and save a loonie. Then, for good measure, I checked our junk drawer and…

Yep. Some plastic cutlery in a little sealed bag. One of those sets we always got when we ordered take-out. We never ended up using them, but we kept them in the drawer as though we might someday remember during some sort of cutlery emergency or something.

Well, that time had come.

I turned back to the kitchen entrance, and then I stopped.

There was no door. It was an open archway. I mean, of course it was. Most kitchens didn't have doors, right? But I wondered if I could get back the same way I'd come. I stepped forward, trying to feel the tug-snap and thinking very, very clearly about the doors in the cafeteria, and…

Nothing.

The rules for where I exited a teleport seemed looser than the rules for where I started.

I blew out a breath. Okay. No time to experiment. I went to my dad's office. It was the closest door, and he never locked it. The moment I touched the door handle, I could feel that pulling sensation. And I wasn't imagining it. It was stronger than before.

I could totally do this.

I closed the door, then opened it, thinking about the cafeteria line-up doors. I'd been through those doors at least once a week for, like, four years now. It was a well-known place. No worries. Easy as anything.

Poof.

A few of the people closest to the door stared as I apologized to Cheri Madison for coming out the in-door and nearly walking right into her—*mental note: be more specific when teleporting*—but Cheri was always super nice, and I'd helped her figure out *plus que parfait* last year so she forgave me. Other than that, I was back at school, no harm done.

I'd take it.

I went back to our table and handed Alec the cutlery. He frowned. "Where'd you get these?"

Right. The cutlery offered at the cafeteria weren't wrapped with little wet-naps and stuff.

"You matter. No second-rate plastic forks for you."

He smiled and opened the packet. Better? He didn't ask any questions.

I cracked my root beer and had a sip.

It tasted like victory.

❖

I didn't see Malik until right at the end of the day, and he was with a group of his friends. He was laughing and he seemed okay, so I forced myself to let it go and grabbed my stuff from my locker. By the time I turned around again, Malik and his friends were gone.

I wished I'd gotten his number. I could have texted him something. Until he texted me, though…

I shook my head.

"You've got serious face."

I turned. Alec had his bag over one shoulder, ready to go.

"Do I?"

"You do. You've had serious face all day. What's up?"

I shook my head. "It's nothing, I think."

"You'd tell me, right?"

I sucked in a breath. *I keep teleporting.* I couldn't force the words past my mouth, though. "I'm working through some unexpected stuff," I said. "Like, really unexpected."

He crossed his arms. "That sounds bad."

"It's…not?" I said, though I hadn't meant for it to come out like a question. "I mean, it's not great, but I think I'm getting a handle on it."

"We're okay, though, right?"

I smiled at him. "We are great. You're my anchor. You're my rock. You're my…my third heavy thing I can't come up with right now because I'm tired."

Alec smiled.

I closed my locker. "Plus side? It's Friday. Date Night at Casa Tozer. My folks will be out being gross parents in love, and I will have sole custody of the house for a whole evening. I can completely let loose, and they will know nothing. I'm thinking of throwing a kegger."

Alec laughed, which had been the point. He shook his head. "Totally. Now what are you really doing?"

"First? I'm gonna take a practice French exam. Then? Biochemical processes. I got a hot date with some YouTube videos that apparently make it super easy to remember how the homeostatic index works."

He grabbed the back of my neck and gave me a little squeeze-shake. "You're out of control, Tozer. Out. Of. Control."

"I'm headed for a life of chaos and fury, for sure."

"In French, even. You want a ride home?"

"You are the best," I said. "The literal best."

"I know it."

We started walking.

"If you want to come over, you can. My folks won't mind. They like you. They always leave me pizza money on Date Night. You can get your homeostatic index on."

"Working tonight," Alec said. "But maybe after, if you *wouldn't mind.*"

"Sure," I said, ignoring the jab. I didn't imagine he'd show. Working with his dad usually meant Alec was exhausted by the time he was done. It was pretty much nonstop lifting at the garage, and even a guy as big as Alec ran out of batteries after schlepping around a few dozen tires or so.

I let Alec go through the doors ahead of me, and I snuck through without touching the door at all. It was much easier to stay put when I didn't actually touch the door itself. The sensation of it pulling at me, though, was still there.

In fact, it was getting stronger even without touching the door. Was that a good sign, or a bad one?

"You've got serious face again," Alec said.

"I'm a serious kind of guy."

"Dude, I know it."

To-Do

- ■ Bring home calculus textbook
- ■ Exam prep: calculus, biology
- ☐ Exam prep: English (reread?)
- ■ Exam prep: French (practice exam!)
- ■ Movie night with Alec this w/e?
- ■ Make lunch for Tuesday, slacker
- ■ "What happened?" joke
- ■ Laundry
- ☐ ~~Slap Malik King~~
- ☐ ~~Doors? DOORS! Definitely Doors.~~
- ■ Alec at RC on Thursday
- ☐ ~~Hungry?~~
- ☐ Calculus: practice derivatives
- ■ Biology: review biochem and metabolic processes
- ■ Bi/Pan?
- ☐ Check in with Sportsball Star?

Cole the Teenage Freak

- ■ ~~Concentrate at doors. All the doors. Every time. You got this!~~
- ☐ Locked doors. One way?
- ☐ Blood sugar? Hungry?
- ☐ CARRY YOUR PHONE.
- ☐ Doors. Again. You don't got this.
- ☐ No door required for exit?
- ☐ Pull getting stronger. Bad? Good?

TWELVE

S o, *do you mind* if I have some popcorn?"
    I sighed. I didn't have to turn and look to know Alec was grinning at me. Ever since I'd stammered and stuttered my way through Malik asking to walk me partway home, Alec had been asking me if I *minded* things. Since Thursday.

This was getting old. But two could play this game.

"Of course," I said, exactly like how I'd waffled with Malik. "I mean, yes. I mean, no. I mean…No popcorn for you." I kept the bowl on my lap.

"Aw, come on." He laughed. "Make with the popcorn."

"Only if you stop making with the mockery." I tried to make one eyebrow go up. I couldn't do it. I probably looked like I was shocked or something.

"Deal," he said, holding out his hand.

I passed him the bowl. He took it and grabbed a handful, then checked his phone again. Not that I was counting, but that was check number six. Since we started the movie. Someone had been texting Alec all night.

Crashed out in comfy clothes on the big ugly couch in my basement and watching a movie was in my top ten ways to spend an evening. Having Alec beside me nudged it into the top five. Normally, I would lean on him while we watched something fun and upbeat if it was my turn to pick or something cute and sweet when it was his turn. Last year, before it had all gone south with Grayson, we'd made the mistake of deciding to share our movie night tradition with him. He'd picked some sort of violent gory horror thing, and that had been the last time we'd tried to widen our movie night bubble.

Tonight, though, we were more than half an hour in and still sitting at either end of the couch. And although I loved this movie—*Beautiful Thing*, which was *super* old, but damn, it sure did make me want a Ste of my own—I was only half paying attention. I had a few things on my mind. Whether or not these two crazy kids would find a way to make it wasn't really getting top billing over the whole "Remember how on Monday I started teleporting and can't seem to make it stop?" thing.

Also? Malik King's questions.

Okay, mostly Malik King's questions. Malik King was definitely getting higher billing than teleportation and cute gay Ste. I should probably be worried about my prioritizing.

Alec and I were halfway through the movie when my phone buzzed. He didn't complain—he couldn't, given how much he'd been fiddling with his own phone the whole time—and I checked. The number wasn't in my contacts.

It had to be Malik.

Hey.

Hey, I sent back. I took a second to set a contact for him, waffling for a moment before settling on a name. *You okay?*

Yeah. Am I interrupting?

No. I'm watching Beautiful Thing *with Alec. Gay classic. We've both seen it a billion times.*

Don't know it. Then, a second later: *Can he see my texts?*

I glanced at Alec, but he was looking at his own phone. Again. *Don't worry. Even if he did I have you listed as Sportsball.* I sent him a screenshot to prove it.

A screenshot came back. He had me in his phone as "Bullet."

My eyebrows rose. *That is the coolest thing anyone has ever called me. If I didn't know it was a reference to my journal, I'd figure you were talking to a gangbanger or something.*

I won't tell if anyone asks.

"Okay, you keep laughing," Alec said. "Who are you talking to?"

"Oh, *I'm* laughing? You've been grinning at your phone since we started the movie."

Alec blushed. *Actually* blushed.

"Wait," I said, holding up my hand. "Am I out of the loop? Is there loop? Have you not looped me in?"

He rolled his eyes. "There's no loop."

"Uh-huh." My phone buzzed again.

I just wanted to say thank you.

It's cool, I wrote. *Any time. I mean it.* I hit Send and stared at Alec. He squirmed.

"Loop," I said.

"Well," he said. "There's this guy."

My mouth dropped open. "Really?"

Alec nodded. His face was so red, he looked sunburned. "We've been chatting a lot. He's ace, too, and we're maybe going to be hanging out."

"That's awesome." I worked hard to make sure it sounded like I meant it. Alec's smile faded. Apparently, I hadn't worked hard enough.

"Really?" he said. "It's felt like a secret, but I've really wanted to tell you and...Really?"

"Really," I said. We weren't saying some stuff here, and I kind of hoped we would keep not saying it, because I'd really hit my limit lately with embarrassing myself in front of people.

"You're okay with it?"

Crap. I was going to have to say things. Sometimes it drove me nuts, but sometimes I really liked how most of my guy friends generally went around not talking about feelings and stuff. That wasn't going to fly tonight, though.

I blew out a breath and paused the movie just as the drag queen was about to meet the boys. "What's his name?" I asked, giving myself time to make words goodly. When I didn't organize my thoughts and plan a response, I got verbal vomit. This could not be a verbal vomit moment.

"Ben."

My phone buzzed again. I glanced at it. *How did your parents react?* I bit my lip. Oy.

"If it's important," Alec said, nodding at my phone.

"It kind of is," I said, cringing. "I do need to answer. But so are you."

He smiled. "Go ahead."

I turned back to my phone. *They were amazing. I mean, they didn't downplay it, and I don't think they were thrilled—I mean, hello, gay kids have extra stuff to worry about, and they were already overprotective, right?—but they weren't mad. They're kind of awesome. Also my dad told me he suspected, but he's basically a mind reader. Are you worried about your parents?*

"Okay," I said, looking at Alec and shifting mental gears. I'd supported my questioning maybe-bi maybe-new-friend, now I needed to support my awesome lifelong best friend. "Are you guys going to maybe do more than hang out?" When Alec frowned, I shook my head. "I didn't mean messing around, I meant…You don't…I know that…" And here came the verbal vomit. Damn it. "You're a cuddler. That's what I mean. You cuddle. We cuddle. Dating, I guess, is what I'm spectacularly failing to say. Is he…Are you both on the same page? I mean, you said some aces aren't into dating at all, right?" Ugh. Could I be any more pathetic? I was totally screwing this up.

But Alec just gave me a slow smile. "I guess it could sort of be a first date," he said. "And you're right. He's not aro. We're similar, from what we've talked about."

"Well, then." I smiled at him. "I repeat, it sounds like it could be awesome."

"Yeah," Alec said. "You're okay?"

My phone buzzed. Of course. I looked down.

Yes. No. Kind of? Huh. Synchronicity. Maybe I could just hold the phone up to Alec and let Malik answer for me.

It buzzed again, and Malik sent me a series of emoji, representing pretty much the whole range of emotions and ending with the one I always thought of as overwhelmed: the smiley face with the little teardrop over its head. *My uncle's gay, so I think my mom will be okay. My grandparents? I dunno. I get the impression they didn't handle it well with my uncle.*

"Yes," I said, looking back up at Alec. "Though movie night is sacred. I hope Ben knows that already."

Alec's relieved smile made my stomach tighten. We'd been friends since we were kids. He'd been the first person I'd come out to, and I'd bawled like a baby. He'd turned around and come out to me right back. He'd been there for me every time I'd managed to find a guy who might have actually liked me back, and had dealt with the fallout of Louis and Brady when it hadn't turned out to be true. I was totally going to be here if Ben turned out to be his shot at the same thing. We'd always be friends, we already knew that. Hell, we'd survived Grayson. We could survive anything.

And I knew being around me wasn't the same as being around someone who felt the way he did. After the crap with Grayson last year, Alec had pulled away from the rest of us for a while, even me, which had hurt. I didn't want to lose him. Not even a little.

I went back to my phone for a second. *Nat always says the best way to guess someone's reaction is to see how they act around other queer people. If your parents are cool with your uncle, that's a really good sign.* I paused. *And you know you don't have to tell them until you want to, right? You get to choose when.* I paused. *Or if.*

"So when's the big date?" I asked, hitting Send.

"Tomorrow night. I'm driving down to meet him."

"Where's he at?"

"Ottawa. He works at a café part time. We're going to hang out."

I smiled at him. "You're nervous."

"I'm freaking out."

"Aww, that's adorable."

Alec rolled his eyes. "I'm not adorable. I'm..." He waved a hand in front of himself. "Big."

Whoa. This wouldn't do. Confidence boosters engaged. "You're a hunk."

He laughed. "Right."

"No, I mean it. You really think Grayson would have chased you like he did if you weren't?"

"Grayson would chase anyone with a pulse."

I shook my head. "That's not true. I mean, okay, I get what you're saying, but it doesn't mean you're not a hunk. You're tall. Your face is a good face. You've got killer eyes." I was tapping off on my fingers. "Also, let's be clear dude, you have *pipes*."

He was blushing again. "Okay, stop."

"Look, if you don't consider Grayson a good enough example, then how about me? We both know I crushed out on you from day one."

He didn't look away, which was...*good*? I could feel my own face burning, but I'd be okay. I wasn't saying anything we didn't both know, and I was past it. Or, y'know, mostly past it. Like, ninety percent. At least. High nineties. It got all confused in my head sometimes because Alec was my best friend and the guy I went to when I needed to talk about anything. Also, if it wasn't for Alec, I'm not sure anyone other than my folks would physically touch me on a regular basis, and how depressing was that? Half the time we watched movies, I ended up kind of leaning against him, or he'd have his arm around me.

Except tonight.

Come to think of it, I maybe relied on Alec as my teddy bear quite a bit when I was needing some comfort or felt completely awkward and undateable, or whenever I was just off balance or feeling out-there.

Like, say, this whole damn week of teleporting and fainting and *especially* the teleporting.

Which, fair is fair, it had been a lot. Who'd blame me wanting a hug?

But we hadn't so much as leaned on each other yet. It struck me this was one of the first times that hadn't happened. And *Beautiful Thing* should totally have brought out the cuddler in Alec.

So what was different?

"I hope..." Alec said, but he stopped.

It felt just a little bit like I was losing something. And maybe I was.

Crap.

"You're my best friend," I said when he didn't finish his sentence. "You're stuck with me. You will be suffering through over-the-top rom coms and musicals for the rest of your life. Popcorn *not* optional."

"Even when you move away?" Alec said.

Well, crap. I was such an idiot.

"I'm going to Ottawa. It's not far. I expect you to visit. Standing date for Movie Nights, mister."

He relaxed visibly. "Thanks." Then he lifted his arm and flicked his fingers. I scooted over, and he wrapped his arm around my shoulder. It felt a bit different there, though. Like, maybe it fit with me better now I wasn't putting something on him that wasn't there.

"So," I said, unpausing the movie. "You got a picture of this Ben?"

"Let me load his Instagram."

I checked my phone while he worked, but Malik didn't reply. I hoped I'd said the right things.

In both conversations.

To-Do

■ Bring home calculus textbook
■ Exam prep: calculus, biology
☐ Exam prep: English (reread?)
■ Exam prep: French (practice exam!)
■ Movie night with Alec this w/e?
■ Make lunch for Tuesday, slacker
■ "What happened?" joke
■ Laundry
☐ ~~Slap Malik King~~
☐ ~~Doors? DOORS! Definitely Doors.~~
■ Alec at RC on Thursday
☐ ~~Hungry?~~
☐ Calculus: practice derivatives—SERIOUSLY, COLE, YOU ARE NOT GOOD AT THIS
■ Biology: review biochem and metabolic processes
■ Bi/Pan?
■ Check in with Sportsball Star?
☐ Follow up with Alec re: his date.
☐ Practice

Cole the Teenage Freak

■ ~~Concentrate at doors. All the doors. Every time. You got this!~~
☐ Locked doors. One way?
☐ Blood sugar? Hungry?
☐ CARRY YOUR PHONE.
☐ Doors. Again. You don't got this.
☐ No door required for exit?
☐ Pull getting stronger. Bad? Good?

THIRTEEN

"Do I talk to you or him?" my dad said, scowling.

He was scary good as an actor, frankly. We were practicing—Terp practice—something we do on Sunday mornings while my mom sleeps in. He runs me through scenarios more or less based on stuff he's done as an interpreter. His ability to slip into a character is pretty awesome. Today? He was pretending to be a doctor he'd visited with a client once. He referred to him as "Dr. Dickhead," and it didn't take me long to see why.

"Him," I said. "I'm just here to interpret."

I was here to interpret for someone getting a check-up over some breathing issues. He was pretty sure he had asthma and was seeing Dr. Dickhead for the follow-up.

The role of the patient was being played by a teddy bear. He didn't talk much.

Despite the stuffie in question being pretty adorable, my father didn't break character. He exhaled and sighed like this was just one more annoyance in his truly overtaxed life of being the most important man in the room. It was a little over-the-top, but it was also fun to see him act like a jerk. I tried not to grin.

"So, the symptoms, your symptoms, the things you were reporting: dizziness, shortness of breath, that—what did you call it—that stitch in your side," my father started, rushing through the words, pretending to talk to the teddy. One part of my brain kept up with the words, another sorted them into ASL syntax, and yet another part of my brain drew forth the signs and worked hard to be clear.

I swear my father only sped up the farther behind I got.

"It's not asthma, and the news isn't good. You're dying."

Whoa.

Then he said something about "metastatic synovial sarcoma," and I lost the thread completely. I stuttered to a stop, my hands froze, and my brain went completely blank. How did you even *spell* synovial?

"Is there a problem?" he said. "Did they get that?" He barked the words at me. He sounded angry. Dr. Dickhead wasn't a dickhead, he was a *complete raging asshole*. He waved his hand in front of my face, and I lowered my hands, defeated.

"That was…" I felt sick. My face burned. "Are you trying to make me screw up?" He'd never done anything like that before. It felt cruel. My dad wasn't cruel.

He leaned forward and gave me patient dad-face. The mask of Dr. Dickhead was gone, just like that. I took a second, and a breath, to try and calm down. Also? I felt like maybe I was about to burst into tears, which was so not good.

Important you know Interpreting can be brutal. He wasn't pretending to be a doctor anymore. Every movement of his hands was gentle, and his face had softened. *Terping isn't easy. I make sure communication happens. Responsibility? Huge!* He paused and spoke. "I become someone's voice, must make sure I'm not talking over them, or add wrong information. Most of the time, I get to be a part of leveling the playing field so Deaf people can help themselves."

I nodded and opened my mouth to tell him that was the whole reason I wanted to do the same thing, but he held up his hand before I could speak.

I closed my mouth and waited. He met my gaze for a few seconds before he went on.

"Sometimes, we must interpret awful things. I interpret for doctors, you know that. I've been the person letting them know they're dying. Or they can't have kids. Or their husband has Alzheimer's. Or sitting there with them while they talk to the police. Your son is missing. Your daughter has been assaulted." He leaned forward. "Sometimes you will be interpreting pain, sorrow, and loss. And you're not there to make it better or protect Deaf people from bad things. You're there to make it clear what someone else said, period. Even when what they said is awful, and how they said it is worse."

I nodded. I remembered days my dad had come home and been distant. And I wasn't dumb. I'd connected those days with him working at the hospital, or the police, or a funeral home. I mean, I'd seen it. I knew that was part of the job. But right now, looking into my dad's eyes and seeing the grief there?

I'd been aware of that part of the job, but I hadn't really *known* it. I felt a little shaky. When I started to sign again, I knew he'd see it. I couldn't hide that kind of stuff from my dad. But I couldn't not ask.

"Is this your way of saying you don't think I'm cut out to be an interpreter?"

His *no* was definitive. He snapped his fingers shut, sharp, pronounced, and clear.

My whole body relaxed. My applications for university were already done. I'd clicked all the buttons and paid the processing fees. University started next September, and I intended to be there, front row center, soaking up as much as I could about linguistics, but the end game had always been certification and then *this*. If I even thought for a second my dad didn't think I could do it?

Well, I had no idea what I'd do.

Okay, I signed.

You've been signing since you were young. You know the culture, and you're smart. I know you can do, my father signed. *I want make sure you know what interpreting is. All of it. Remember: it's not the only thing in the world.*

"Okay," I said again, feeling a little less stable. Of course it wasn't the only job. But it was the only job I'd imagined having.

He leaned back. Then he grinned. *Also remember we interpreted for couple who thought they couldn't have kids. Surprise! Twins. There are good times, too.*

I smiled. "That sounds awesome."

He nodded. *True work.* He regarded me, his dad-vision reengaged. *Ready for more?*

"Yes." I didn't want to end on that failure. But I made a mental note to spend some time later finding out what some of the signs were for diseases and illnesses I'd never had a reason to learn.

Okay, my dad signed. *This time, I'll be the client. Another patient-doctor job. You interpret for the patient.* He looked back at his computer, scrolling through his files the way he did to trigger a memory of some random job he'd done, and then stopped at one. He clapped his hands and laughed.

Uh-oh.

When he faced me, his whole manner transformed. He sort of curled into himself and bit his bottom lip. He wouldn't look at me and kept his eyes low. Then he started signing with zero mouthing, in pure ASL. He'd code switched on me. Tricky man, but if I was interpreting,

I'd need to know what I was doing regardless of whether or not someone was using ASL or Signed English. I shifted mental gears and watched him sign about a *really* itchy rash that was spreading "down there."

This time? I managed to keep my face blank, but it was only just.

❖

Dad had to go for a meeting with a client after lunch, and Mom was doing laundry, so I went back to my room and flipped open my bullet journal. And right there, at the end of the list, was the thing I'd written down yesterday once Alec had left.

Practice.

I exhaled and looked at my bedroom door. After Friday's accidental kitchen rebound, I hadn't tripped up once going through any doors. Becoming hyper-aware of where all the doors were wasn't exactly easy, but my mom always said it only took a week to make a good habit. As of tomorrow, I could celebrate my first official week as a teleporting freak.

I closed my bedroom door, aware of the pull I could feel the moment my hand was on the handle. It was like that every time now. It helped remind me, helped me keep my guard up, but...

I sighed and let go.

I wanted to reread *The Wars* for English. Maybe I could kill two birds with one stone. I grabbed the book, my phone, and my bullet journal and went downstairs.

"You okay on your own?" I asked my mom. She was sitting on the couch, reading a book. Her feet were up, and a cup of coffee was cooling on the table beside her. Sundays were her quiet days, most of the time.

"Somehow I'll manage," she said. She could be kind of sarcastic on the weekends. I think she stored it up all week because she couldn't release it on the patients. "You heading out?"

"I have a hot date with *The Wars*. Figured I'd reread it before the exam, because I hated it."

"That's not normally why people reread books."

"It's possible I did a lot of skimming and used YouTube."

"So, not so much a *reread* as a *read*, then?" She picked up her coffee and sipped it, looking over it at me in her distinctly "mom" way. Jennifer Tozer, dental hygienist, was off the clock. Mom Tozer, on the other hand...

"Guilty," I said. "So I will be out and reading. Have my phone, have my keys."

"Where are you going to be?"

Crap. I needed her to not pin down one spot, because practice was also on the menu. She put down her coffee and picked up her book again, waiting for me to reply. The cover of her book was black and had red writing along with an outline of a figure in chalk.

"I'll try the café first," I said. Brenda's Café was at the far end of Main near the library, but everyone just called it "the café." "If it's quiet enough there, I'll stick around." That gave me an out. And now, to spring a distraction. "Do you ever read an author named Wallace?"

"Do you mean Dita Wallace?"

I shrugged. "I'm not sure. I don't remember her first name. This guy at school? His mom writes mysteries. Apparently, she won a...I want to say Edward? Some kind of award."

"An Edgar?" My mom's eyebrows rose. Together. She, like her progeny, couldn't isolate eyebrows for lifting. In a weird way, it gave me a warm and snuggly feeling. Check us out. Related after all.

"Yeah, that."

"Honey, I've read *all* of her books. Is this a good friend? Would this friend introduce me to his mother?" She was leaning forward. "Her detective is fantastic. And the books are *hot*."

"I can ask," I said, holding up a hand because I didn't want to hear more about how hot the books were. Were mysteries supposed to be hot? Never mind. Doubling down on not wanting to hear more.

"Child of the year," she said.

"Three years running," I said, and I was free.

Mom couldn't see the front door from where she was sitting, so I left her reading and took a second to gather my thoughts while I stood there. The rest of today I'd reread—okay, fine, *read*—The Wars, but every time my attention wandered I'd pick somewhere new to go read it. And I'd get there the freak way.

I grabbed the front door and thought about the café.

Tug.

Snap.

Poof.

To-Do

- ☑ Bring home calculus textbook
- ☑ Exam prep: calculus, biology
- ☑ Exam prep: English (reread?)
- ☑ Exam prep: French (practice exam!)
- ☑ Movie night with Alec this w/e?
- ☑ Make lunch for Tuesday, slacker
- ☑ "What happened?" joke
- ☑ Laundry
- ☐ ~~Slap Malik King~~
- ☐ ~~Doors? DOORS! Definitely Doors.~~
- ☑ Alec at RC on Thursday
- ☐ ~~Hungry?~~
- ☐ Calculus: practice derivatives—SERIOUSLY, COLE, YOU ARE NOT GOOD AT THIS
- ☑ Biology: review biochem and metabolic processes
- ☑ Bi/Pan?
- ☑ Check in with Sportsball Star?
- ☐ Follow up with Alec re: his date.
- ☑ Practice

Cole the Teenage Freak

- ☑ ~~Concentrate at doors. All the doors. Every time. You got this!~~
- ☐ Locked doors. One way?
- ☑ Blood sugar? Hungry? Definitely hungry.
- ☐ CARRY YOUR PHONE.
- ☐ Doors. Again. You don't got this.
- ☐ No door required for exit?
- ☐ Pull getting stronger. Bad? Good?

Fourteen

The same bearded man from last week was creeping me out as I went to my locker. I tried a casual glance behind me, which was probably super obvious. Sure enough, he was standing just at the entrance to the music room. Watching me.

I turned back to my locker. My arm hair was rising, and unless I was mistaken, this was the same substitute teacher who'd thought it was a joy to stare at me across the track field. Was I crazy? Was I manufacturing some sort of paranoid delusion?

Was I having a Colenap Stranger Danger moment?

I shuddered, a full-body shiver that felt an awful lot like the tug-and-snap I was getting used to every time I walked through a door without teleporting. I panicked and closed my eyes. *No. No no no.* My heart hammered in my chest, and I held on to my locker with a death grip. I opened my eyes slowly...but I was still in the hallway by my locker.

I hadn't teleported. I was right here. Hadn't gone anywhere.

It was bad enough with the whole "every door is potentially dangerous" thing. If it turned out anxiety could make me teleport *without* a door, I was well and truly fucked.

This was so unfair. Yesterday had been good for my confidence with this whole teleporting thing. I didn't need another problem. I'd popped all over town. *The Wars* was *so* boring, by the time I'd finished it, I'd only had one misfire out of maybe ten teleports. When I aimed for Meeples, I'd ended up in Meeples's bathroom rather than the front of the store. Part of why I'd wanted to go to Meeples was because I needed the bathroom, though, so as mistakes went, it was a time-saver.

Also, I'd been starving and desperately wanted a lemon bar. Teleporting definitely burned calories. Way better than exercise, too. That was a plus.

But random teleporting *without* doors whenever I freaked out? Not down for that.

Also not down for creepy teachers who stare.

I turned to glance again, unable to help myself, but Beardy McBeardface was gone. My relief was palpable.

I'd slept like crap, full of nightmares about showing up naked in strange places, which was all the more terrifying now it could actually happen, and I'd gotten up before my alarm clock had even started to change from red to orange. I'd made coffee for my parents and had even had time for a bowl of cereal before it was time to get ready. Even better, I'd scored a ride with my mom. Once I'd gotten to school and realized I was here before anyone I generally talked to, however, it felt less awesome and more boring.

Now I was glad to be so early. I could potentially calm myself down before people arrived for the day. I knelt down and grabbed my books, and when I stood back up, I couldn't help but glance at the music room again. The door was closed.

"I downloaded your movie," Malik said. He was right beside me.

I jumped, and he laughed. Guy was a freaking ninja.

"Sorry," he said.

"I didn't hear you coming." Captain Obvious.

He nodded, still grinning at me. I replayed what he'd said, but it didn't click.

"My movie?"

"*Beautiful Thing*," Malik said, lowering his voice.

I stopped, really looking at him. He looked different today. Normally, Malik had this kind of casual "I don't care, but it totally works on me" look to how he dressed I envied but couldn't duplicate. Today, though? Was it just me, or had I never before seen him wearing something other than a T-shirt? Even in winter, I generally got to enjoy the way T-shirts fit Malik King.

Snug, by the way. T-shirts fit Malik *snug*.

Today, he was wearing a hoodie, which didn't feel very Malik to me. Not that I had any business defining what *was* Malik or not.

"You good?" I said. That was as close to breaking the guy code as I could get. Y'know. Feelings and stuff. No talking about those. He hadn't texted me again at all for the rest of the weekend, and I totally hadn't stopped each and every time I teleported all around town to check my phone just in case he had checked in. Nope. Not at all.

"Yeah." He stuffed his hands in the hoodie pocket, like he wanted to put all of himself in there, and he glanced over my shoulder.

Shit. I knew that look. I tried to bite down some disappointment and reminded myself that Malik had every right to be concerned about being seen talking to me. Hell, no doubt Austin had already lambasted him for catching him talking to me just that one time at lunch.

Malik saw me notice him look, and he winced. He twisted his hands in the hoodie pocket. Maybe hoodies were Malik's version of my big grey sweater. If so? Comfort mode wasn't activating.

"Did you like it?" I said, to break the moment.

It was Malik's turn not to follow. He frowned.

"The movie."

"Oh," Malik said, then he smiled again. "It was okay. Old. I mean, it was good, though."

"I like to imagine Jamie runs a pub of his own now, and Ste is a lifeguard," I said.

"You think?" Malik frowned. "I figured after they moved, it would've been too hard for them to stay together."

I considered that but shook my head. "The nice thing about movies is you get to have happy endings. I mean, sure, they struggle with the long-distance thing, and Jamie is tempted by some of the other guys he gets to meet, but once Ste finishes his courses and Jamie's done with school, they end up living together."

Malik blinked. "You've really thought this through."

"It's a game Alec and I play. 'What happens next?'"

"Huh," Malik said. He looked around again. Checking.

Okay. This was the part where I needed to be a better queer. I could almost hear Nat's voice reminding me to be accommodating and understanding and to have empathy. Malik came first. The fact he was making me feel like a leper wasn't his fault. It was our stupid culture and the stupid homophobia, and that didn't make it suck any less, but the important thing here was being supportive.

"You don't have to hang out with me," I said. "If you're not feeling comfortable, I mean. I'm totally okay with you texting. Or if you want to talk, we could hang out somewhere else. Meeples, maybe. I don't see many people you know there, ever."

Malik's face fell, but I couldn't tell if it was guilt or relief. Or both. "I'm sorry."

I shook my head. "Don't be. I legit mean it. It's okay. I get it. Guilt by association is not going to make any of this easier on you, no matter what you decide to do. So go hang out with your friends. I'm here if you need me. I've always got my phone." I held it up.

Malik nodded, and I tried not to be stung by the obvious win of relief over guilt. "Thanks. And yeah, if we could hang out, maybe at Meeples, that would be cool. I like you."

I tried *heroically* not to overreact to that particular statement. I failed. Immediate giant-ass stupid grin on my face.

"Okay," I said. "Let me know when you're free." I held up my phone again, in case he'd forgotten in the last few seconds that I had one.

He nodded, then turned to go. Two steps away, though, he pivoted. "Y'know, Alec is a lucky guy."

Then he was gone.

I frowned. Alec was a lucky guy? What did that…?

Oh.

I turned around and closed my locker.

Malik thought I was dating Alec. Why would he think…?

Well, there was the whole watching movies together thing, and the more I thought about it, I sure did hang out with Alec a lot, didn't I? And on Thursday, when Alec had offered me a ride home from Meeples, I'd said what I always said.

"Kisses."

Well, hell.

❖

I scored the last available tree and had a bite of my sandwich before I texted Alec.

At the trees.

Give me five, he sent a second later. It was more like ten, but he showed up with a paper plate and a stack of three slices of pizza from the cafeteria line, so no doubt he'd been waiting for food.

He joined me, leaning back against the tree and taking a big bite. He didn't unstack the slices first. He grunted.

"Hungry?" I said.

"Very," he said, around a mouth full of food.

"So, you gonna make me ask or you gonna volunteer?"

He chewed, but he nodded. When he finally swallowed, he said, "It was okay."

"Just okay?"

He nodded. "Remember your date with Louis?"

I winced. "Uh-oh. Did Ben turn out to be full of himself?"

Alec shook his head. "No. Not that. But it was more like *practice*. Ben is nice. We'll definitely hang out some, and it was so great to talk to him about some things, but..." He took another bite, chewed, swallowed. "We haven't got much in common, I guess."

"Ah," I said. That was like me and Louis. I mean, beyond working at the Deaf camp and both being of the opinion that there were boys worth making out with, it had turned out we didn't share much else. Well, apart from sharing the opinion that Louis was really cute, but that turned out to not be the basis of a scintillating conversation.

Alec shrugged. "It was okay. I mean, we got to vent, which was cool."

"By 'vent' I'm guessing you mean Grayson?"

"And all those like him." Alec nodded.

I took a breath. "He seems to be working at it a bit. I mean, no excuses, and you know where I stand, but lately?" I shrugged.

Alec grunted, but it wasn't a complete disagreement, so I let it go. He had to have noticed, too. He didn't have to forgive Grayson all the crap he'd said about Alec not being queer enough, but it seemed like Grayson had at least clued in he'd been wrong. Was that progress? It still drove me mental that Alec didn't come to the club meetings and Grayson did. It was like Alec had decided Grayson was right.

Maybe Nat had had another talk with Grayson. That might explain his change of attitude. If there was one. I hoped there was one.

"What about you?" Alec said.

I didn't follow. "What about me?"

Alec looked at me for a few seconds, then said, "Is there loop?"

I shook my head. "I've decided this year I'm totally going to talk to Hot Kanata Guy, if he shows up at the end-of-year thing." I tried to make it sound convincing, but the truth was it wasn't particularly something I cared about. Still, it was a decent goal.

"I think Grayson might beat you to it."

"Maybe that should be my technique. Offer myself up as a Plan B once Grayson is talking to him," I said. "Give him an out."

Alec's eyes widened. "Dude. That's borderline genius."

"I am not just a pretty face," I said.

Alec grinned. His pizza was almost gone. It was like a magic trick. When the final bit of the third crust vanished, he shifted against the tree and closed his eyes. "Wake me up before the bell rings."

"Got it," I said.

❖

After school, I checked my phone and considered my options. I really, really needed to put in more study time. The most diligent thing I could do would be to rejig my study schedule and get down to some quality time with my notes. I needed to remind myself how derivatives worked. We'd spent weeks on it in class. I was pretty sure it would be on the exam.

It didn't really belong on my top five list of favorites, but I took a deep breath and grabbed my bag and my books.

The ping on my phone was so welcome, I was smiling before I even saw who sent the message.

The screen said *Sportsball.*

I thumbed my phone and checked the message, grinning.

Heading to Meeples?

On some instinct, I looked up. Malik was there with Jacob and Tyler, and they were obviously doing their goodbyes, what with the endless complicated handshakes no one had ever attempted with me. Which was good. Because I'd probably put someone's eye out or punch myself. I noticed he had his phone in his free hand.

He'd also lost the hoodie.

I smiled at the return of Malik-in-a-T-shirt, and typed a quick response.

Definitely. I intend to study, and it's the best place to study, ever. Or at least, it would be. I supposed. Normally, I only went there to play games, but I'm sure Candice wouldn't mind if I was studying.

I wrote a message to my parents. *Just so you know, I'm going to study at Meeples with a friend.* I wasn't asking for permission, exactly, but I knew it would fly better if I looped them in. Me not coming home after school would result in ever-escalating texts and phone calls if I didn't check in. Better to send off prior warning.

Malik replied right after I sent the text to my parents.

I can crash it?

I sent him a thumbs-up emoji. Then I watched him look at his phone, and I have to admit, it was sort of fun to watch him react to the little ping sound and know I was the one who sent it. Although it wasn't a ping. It was some sort of riff of notes that I'd never heard before. It was borderline metal. I imagined the little message bubble popping up from "Bullet" with that noise, and I had never felt cooler.

He smiled at his phone, finished his goodbyes with his friends, and typed again.

See you there.

I grabbed my stuff, and if I was moving faster than I had before, it was because I intended to master derivatives and ace my exams.

Totally.

❖

Candice brought me my hot chocolate and my lemon bar, and I'd finished half of both before the little bell on the door turned out to be Malik. He did this nod-and-smile thing in my direction, and I waved my fingers at him in this totally casual way that would have been so much more effective if I hadn't knocked my fork off my plate in the process.

By the time I got over being mortified and got my cutlery back under control, he was sitting down across from me. He put down his backpack and pulled out a binder and his textbook.

"How are you at world history?" He sounded hopeful.

"Nope." I shook my head. "Sorry. I left history behind as soon as I could."

He sighed. "Smart. What are you doing?"

"Mostly? I'm trying to remember why I thought calculus was a good idea."

He grimaced. "Ugh. You can have it. I'll stick to history."

"Right?"

Candice came over. "Study night?"

"Exams soon," I said. "This is Malik."

"You were here the other night," Candice said. "I remember. Did you like the lemon bar?"

"It was epic," he said. "But Cole said I should try the date square. And may I have a mocha, please?"

"Coming right up," Candice said. "You still good, Cole?"

"Yes, thanks."

Malik was quiet for a second, then he reached out and tapped my bullet journal. "So, is this the gun book?"

I could feel my face getting hot. My bullet journal wasn't like some of the ones I'd seen online. I didn't go crazy with washi tape or anything, but it was still a bullet journal. "Yeah." And then, because it felt kind of like I should, I flipped it open to the bookmark of the latest to-do page I was working through. "Behold me in all my nerdy glory."

He looked. "So, it's mostly to-do lists?"

"Sort of. It's a system. It's streamlined. You don't start over every day so much as you keep going. There's eighteen lines, so until you need to turn a page you don't rewrite anything. I'm at the bottom of the page now with this one, so tomorrow, if I add another, it's like starting fresh."

The more I spoke, the less cool I sounded. I let it drop. Candice came back with his square and his mocha, and winked at me. I had no idea what that meant, but since Malik was still looking at my journal and I'm just that much of a geek, I explained how the index worked, the calendar pages, the various lists I kept track of favorites and stuff I wanted to remember. I tried not to stutter while he flipped the book around to face him—I hadn't expected him to *really* look.

He lifted his gaze. "Check in with Sportsball Star?"

Oops. Right. I shrugged. "Like I said, I'm a nerd."

He looked back down at the list again. I reached over and turned the pages back until…There. "See? The Louvre." My top five lists page. Places I'd been. Places I wanted to go. Favorite books. Favorite movies. "Behold my sad glory."

"Hey, did you draw this?" Malik said, turning the journal back around. It was just a sketch I'd drawn of the glass pyramid in front of the Louvre, and it had turned out pretty well. I'd copied it off a picture I'd found online.

"Sort of," I said. "I had a photo I was looking at."

"You can draw," he said.

"I like to draw. I had art last semester." I shrugged. "But I can only draw stuff I'm looking at. I can't do it from memory or anything."

"I can't even do stick figures."

"Yeah, but you can put the sportsball into the point-scoring areas."

He laughed. He took a bite of his date square and made a little grunting noise.

"Do I lie," I said. "Or is that an epic date square?"

He nodded, chewing.

I closed my bullet journal and leaned back in my chair. My binder was open, as was my textbook, but frankly the last thing I cared about at that moment was derivatives. Malik finished his date square and opened his own book. Not only had his hoodie returned, he shoved his hands into the pocket while he read, I noticed, only pulling one out to turn the page when he needed to.

Okay. Ignore the hoodie—also the cute boy in the hoodie—and get to work.

We studied for a while. I don't know how much sank into my head, but I made it through my notes and did a couple of problems and achieved the correct answer, so I was calling it a win. After I checked one and saw I'd gotten the third correct answer in a row, I heard a little snort and looked up to see Malik staring at me. It looked like he was trying not to laugh.

"What?" I said.

"When you get one right, you cheer for yourself."

With horror, I realized he was right. I'd been making little applause noises under my breath, like a cheering crowd, every time I got a problem right. This was why I didn't study in public. I had no idea what to say or do. Maybe I could tip my chair over backward and knock myself out.

"Sorry. I'll try to keep it down. Some of us aren't routinely cheered on sportsball fields and have to make our own fans."

He laughed. He actually laughed. If only Grayson were here to witness me telling a joke.

I took the last swallow of my not-even-a-little-bit-hot chocolate and glanced at my phone. Holy crap. We'd been here for an hour already. Time flew when you were bored to tears. I looked around and saw people playing games at a couple of the tables. I'd tuned them out, and even if Monday nights weren't exactly super-happening at Meeples, Candice seemed to be moving around with purpose.

"Can I ask you something?" Malik said.

I nodded.

"Does it ever...bother you?" he said. "Being..." He didn't finish the sentence.

I took a deep breath. I knew what he meant, of course. I wasn't sure if there was a right answer. I was pretty sure I knew what Nat would say. *If in doubt? Honesty.* "Sometimes, yes."

He looked surprised.

I shrugged. "Not in a 'I wish I wasn't gay' way. Not that. Just..." I tried to find the right words. "It's the little stuff, I guess. I mean, okay, also all the big stuff, but that's obvious. The little stuff is more exhausting cause it's all the time."

He shook his head.

"Okay, examples. Last year? I went on a date with this guy. Louis. He was at Deaf camp with me, another counsellor. We could go into town on some of the weekends, kind of like a day off, and we organized one together after he found out I thought he was cute and he agreed that he was cute."

Malik's eyebrow slid up. "So, he was humble."

"A world of no. But it was a good practice for a real date, I guess. At least, that's what I tell myself. And we did have fun. Just a coffee shop and then a walk around the town. Nothing major, right?"

Malik nodded.

"Except when we were in the coffee shop, the barista was watching us sign. We'd drawn attention, I guess. I was laughing a lot. Louis was funny. Anyway, when we were bringing over the cups once we were done, she sort of looked right through him and asked me, 'Are you guys brothers?'"

"Did he look like you?"

"Ha! No. I guess I wasn't clear when I say he was *cute*." I shrugged. "No, I don't get how anyone would think we were related. He's blond and tall and has these amazing pretty eyes. Basically the whole checklist for the cover of some magazine. I am none of those things. But she asked, and it was really, really awkward. Like, first off she'd done that audist thing where she talked right past Louis like he was some sort of broken puppy."

Malik shook his head. "Sorry, audist?"

"Hearing people do all sorts of stuff that's just rude and dismissive of Deaf people. That's the word for it. Audist. Like racist, or sexist, or whatever."

"Ah."

"So, first there was that," I said. "Louis had no idea she'd said anything, and I was standing there thinking, 'Do I out us?' Like, she asked if we were brothers, so I had a built-in option to just agree. I could say we were, because who cares, right? Except I *do* care. I mean, I'm not as vocal as Grayson, but I care. So I said, 'No, we're on a date.'"

"Okay."

I shook my head. "Not okay. She got all embarrassed. Like, she started stuttering out this half-ass apology. By then, Louis noticed something was going on, and he was asking me what she'd said, and I'm trying to sign some sort of précis of her verbal vomit, and she flips out all over again because she doesn't know what I'm signing to him, and now she thinks I'm badmouthing her. 'I don't judge people, you can be anything and love anyone and that's okay by me,' and so on. She was so loud. The rest of the customers were staring." I shook my head. "It was so awkward. We got out of there, and we took our walk, but the whole time I was thinking about it. It's stuff like that that bugs me. Like, the constant assumption I'm not something different until I say so, which means I have to choose to say so, which means it's all on me. Does that make sense?"

He nodded again. "Sounds familiar."

"It does?"

"Where are you from?" Malik said, in a chipper voice that could have been mocking pretty much anyone. "If I say 'Toronto,' it's like people think I'm lying. They'll say, 'No, I mean *before.*'"

"Ouch," I said.

He shrugged. "It's a thing. Sometimes I say Wakanda. People pretend to know it."

I gaped. "You're kidding."

He shook his head. "Not even a little."

I crossed my arms over my chest. "My king."

He laughed. Then he sighed. "I miss Toronto."

"I don't blame you. This place is small. But! We're almost done with it, and you can go anywhere you want after. Toronto, even."

"You have this bright-side outlook, you know that?"

"Relentless optimism. It's my thing."

"Really?"

I shook my head. "No. Not even a little bit. But it sounded better than 'I can't wait to get out of this town, either.'"

Another eyebrow. Between the brown eyes and the smile and the eyebrow thing, it took me a second to remember to breathe. It was *so* wrong to crush out on him when he was just kinda-sorta coming out. So wrong. But the *eyebrow.*

"Why do you want to leave?" he said.

"Mostly? Colenap. I'd like to be somewhere where nobody knows about Colenap."

"Ah."

"And to further answer your question, also I'd like to be somewhere where I can kiss a guy without checking over my shoulder first," I said. "I mean, not that this place is bad, but self-defense classes or not, I'm no Black Panther. Or Captain America. I'm pretty sure I'm not even Bruce Banner." I shook my head. "Honestly, I'm not sure there's a real place like that. Yet. Anyway."

"The Village," Malik said. "Church, Yonge."

"See? Toronto. It's the place to be."

"What about Louis?" Malik asked. "Any…kissing?"

Okay. He'd kind of stuttered there and it was awkward, but it was also adorable that he asked. I shook my head. "Not really. We just had that one date. I mean, yeah, there was *a* kiss, but…Meh? He has a girlfriend now."

The eyebrow rose again.

"I keep telling you," I said. "Boys and girls. It's allowed."

He bit his lip.

"What?" I said, readying more support for the existence of bisexuals. I'd done my homework. I didn't have any sports-type heroes to suggest, but I had a whole list of actors and actresses. *You get to feel how you feel*, I thought. *It's allowed. You're allowed.*

Something *happened*. He looked up quickly, like I'd just said something, but I hadn't. Goosebumps broke out across my skin.

I swallowed.

That…What was that?

Malik blinked, like he'd lost his train of thought, nodding at my journal. "It said to check on Alec and his date?"

"Oh. Yeah." Conversational whiplash. Man. Maybe I shouldn't have flashed my to-do lists at him. It struck me he hadn't looked farther than my latest to-do list page, which was good. The flip side had my ongoing issues with teleportation list. That would have been problematic to explain. Also, I was glad I'd scribbled though my note to myself to give him a slap.

"I thought…" he said.

I shook my head. It wasn't my place to out Alec's asexuality, but I could definitely be clear that we weren't dating. "No. He's my best friend. Since we were kids."

He nodded.

"Refills?" Candice said, coming by with perfect timing.

"Yes, please," I said, and Malik echoed me. She took our cups away.

Malik smiled again, and then he got back to his history textbook. I went back to calculus, though for a good long while I wasn't even aware of derivatives. Truth be told, I was thinking about dates and kisses and what was fast becoming the world's cutest eyebrow.

❖

"Okay," Candice said, coming over to wipe the table. "Dish."

Malik had left. I'd waffled over asking him if he wanted company on the walk home and hadn't offered, which I now regretted. He'd done this thing where he'd patted my shoulder as he left and now I was wondering if I was a complete idiot, or just shy of all the pieces.

"Sorry?" I said, snapping back.

"Boy is cute. Boy is sitting with you for two hours, and sneaking looks at you when you're not looking at him. Dish."

"What?" My voice did this squeaky thing. "No. He's...I mean. Really? Are you sure?"

"Aw, honey." Candice laughed at me.

"It's just...He's really cool," I said, trying to explain. "He's, like, one of the best athletes at school." I couldn't express this clearly enough. "When he throws balls, they go where he wants them to. I think schools are willing to give him money because he does it so well."

"Wow," Candice said. Her lips were kind of wiggling. I didn't think she was treating this information with the correct level of respect. "I guess that makes him royalty, then?"

"He's a friend," I said. "Trust me." But I could feel my skin getting hot. Who was I trying to convince here?

"Cole," Candice said. "I couldn't hear everything he was saying, but I heard some of it. Do me a favor. Ask yourself if you think he has those conversations with his other friends. Or if he'd hang out with them for a couple of hours in my shop. Doing *homework*."

Then she patted my arm and was gone.

Yeah. So that just happened.

I packed up, paid up, and paused at the door long enough to wave. I had to concentrate hard on not going anywhere but outside. It worked, and I started the walk home.

This door thing was not getting better. This time it felt like little popping fireworks were on the other side of Meeples's door. God only knew what that meant, and I so didn't want to find out. Also, had Candice really just suggested that Malik—?

A full-body shudder hit me so hard it made me stop walking. It wasn't someone walking over my grave so much as it was someone leading a parade there. My heart jacked up to a hummingbird pace. Something was *wrong*. Something was *very* wrong.

I slid my hand into my pocket and grabbed my phone. As casually as I could, I pretended I'd just gotten a text or something, then pulled up the camera. I counted to five, skin still crawling, then turned around, lifted the phone, and took a bunch of pictures.

To his credit, the guy with the beard didn't run away or anything. He just stood in front of Meeples, watching me take his photo.

When I finally lowered my phone, he turned and walked away in the other direction.

"Okay," I said. "Officially freaking out."

I looked at my phone. None of the shots were great, but if I zoomed in enough, at least I could tell he was the same man from at school. I turned off the phone and headed for home. This wasn't Colenap Stranger Danger spidey-sense gone awry.

That man was following me.

To-Do

☐ Bearded rando. Sub? Talk to principal?

Cole the Teenage Freak

■ ~~Concentrate at doors. All the doors. Every time. You got this!~~
☐ Locked doors. One way?
■ Blood sugar? Hungry? Definitely hungry.
☐ CARRY YOUR PHONE.
☐ Doors. Again. <u>You don't got this</u>.
☐ No door required for exit?
☐ Pull getting stronger. Bad? Good?
☐ Popping thing. Like fireworks.

FIFTEEN

I kept it to two snoozes and hopped into the shower more or less on time. I'd had a crappy night's sleep, my head racing from one thing to another until I finally crashed out somewhere around two in the morning, and now I was feeling it. The shower helped, so I let the water beat on my face for a few minutes longer, then I turned it off and started drying myself.

I didn't really know what to do about Beardy McBeardface. I mean, sure, he wigged me out, and last night he was one of the things I'd been overthinking. I'd come to the conclusion I didn't exactly have a lot to go on. I mean, he looked at me. That wasn't exactly a crime, right? But it was creepy. I thought about telling my parents for roughly a millisecond before common sense reminded me they were likely to overreact to the nth over any potential threat, so that was out.

When I wasn't thinking about Beardy McBeardface, I was thinking about my teleporting problem. By this point, it was more frustrating and annoying than weird, which in and of itself felt like something I should worry about.

And when I wasn't thinking about my teleporting problem, I was thinking about a certain eyebrow and the boy said eyebrow was attached to.

So, yeah, no sleep. Grumpy Cole Tozer was in the house.

Though it *was* fun thinking about Malik.

"Stop," I said, wrapping the towel around my waist. "He's not even out. You can't crush out on him. You can't."

I stepped out of the shower—

Poof.

—and into a shower.

I nearly fell, my foot landing higher than I expected, but I kept my balance. Just. The tiles were blue, not white. Also, the shower stall was smaller, and the glass door was frosted in a different pattern and the towel hanging over it wasn't one I'd seen before and…

Where the *hell* was I now?

Like I said, way more frustrating and annoying than weird.

I bit my lip. I was wearing a towel. I was in a strange bathroom I didn't recognize. Apparently, now even my own glass door on my own shower was a problem. I wanted to scream, but that was out of the question given I had no freaking idea where I was.

Plus side? My exit plan was obvious. I reached for the door, ready to head back home as fast as I could, when someone started humming.

In the bathroom. With me.

I froze.

A couple of words, then more humming.

I closed my eyes, recognizing the voice. Of course. What had I been thinking about when I was getting out of the shower?

Malik King. I was in his bathroom. And so was he. I was trapped in his shower. In a towel.

Well, I couldn't do anything about it now. I took hold of the glass door, crouching to hide as much of myself behind the hanging towel as I could. I needed to be quick. Just push the door open and teleport the heck out of here.

I could do this.

I saw the shadow of two legs appear at the bottom of the glass, beneath the towel, and had to bite down on a shriek.

I pushed, and I let the tug grab me the second I felt it. *Home.* I thought. *Home, home, home.* Shower to shower. Glass door to glass door. Malik yelped as I pushed the glass door open.

Poof.

I ended up where I wanted. Generally. Yes, I was inside my house. But I was in front of the back patio. Because glass door I guess? *Ha ha, thank you universe.* I snuck back upstairs in my towel without my mom or dad seeing me, which was pretty much the only thing going right in the moment. I got to my bedroom and sat down hard on my bed.

No way Malik could have seen me, right? I mean, I was crouched, and a towel was in the way on the door and I teleported and *there was no way he could have seen me.* I fell back on my blanket, panting like I'd run a marathon.

Then it hit me: *I'd never been to Malik's house.*

Until now, I'd only teleported places I'd already been.

My list of things that could go wrong with this whole teleporting thing? It just got a whole lot worse.

"If anyone's listening," I said, staring up at the ceiling. "I am at my limit, okay? No need to dial it up any more. I could really, really use a break right now. Something to go my way? That would be great."

Someone knocked on my door. I jumped.

"You want a ride to school?" It was my mother.

"Really?" I glared upward. "That's the best you can come up with?"

"What was that? Didn't hear you," my mother said.

"Yes, please," I said, louder. "I just need a second to get dressed."

❖

As soon as I got to school, I grabbed my stuff for class and then slipped into my homeroom. Dodging the pull of the door wasn't so bad, and I barely had to work to stay put. Whether or not that was progress, I wasn't sure. I might have just used up all my accidental teleporting gas this morning. Maybe it was harder to teleport somewhere I'd never been. Maybe I'd end up inside a maximum security jail cell with a sociopathic murderer the next time I wasn't paying attention.

I was panting again. I took a second by the door to calm down, trying to remind myself to deal with one thing at a time. But I couldn't help it. Would I ever get this figured out, or was I doomed to end up haunting the bathrooms of other people who happened to have glass shower doors?

Stop it. One disaster at a time, Cole. Stick to the plan.

Mr. Jones was the only other person in the room, which suited me just fine. He was writing something down, but he looked up as I got to his desk.

"Hey, Cole," he said. "What's up?"

"The substitute teacher," I said. "Is he still here?"

Mr. Jones frowned. "Substitute teacher?"

I nodded, though a slick, oily feeling started to pool in my stomach. "Tall. Beard. I'm sorry, I don't know his name."

But he was already shaking his head. "As far as I know, there's no substitute here today. Why?"

"It's just..." I took a breath. "It might sound stupid, but...he stares."

Mr. Jones put his pen down, a line forming between his eyebrows. I had his full attention now. "When was this?"

I could have cheered. Mr. Jones was my favorite teacher for a reason. I had him for English as well as homeroom, and he *listened*. Like, *really* listened. Also, I could totally tell it would give him pleasure to boot Austin in the ass. I mean, he *wouldn't*, but he *wanted* to, and that made all the difference.

He also mentioned his husband sometimes, which, y'know, score one for team queer.

"Last week," I said. "Out in the hall by the music room, but also out by the field at lunch. Grayson saw him, too. I don't know his name. I haven't had him for any classes, but..." I shrugged. "I keep seeing him and he...*stares*."

"Last week." Mr. Jones's frown grew. "And he made you uncomfortable?"

And how. "A little."

"Let me find out," he said.

"Thank you," I said, relieved. I thought about telling him I'd seen him downtown, too, but I didn't want to push it. I could bring that up later, once I had a name other than Beardy McBeardface to work with. Besides, it sounded like maybe he wasn't around anymore, which was awesome.

Some other kids started coming into the class, so I went to my desk. I opened my bullet journal and colored in the little square beside the task, and then flipped back a page to where my other big problem grew by one more item.

A potentially sociopathic serial killer in a small space problem.

Or, on the other hand, cute boys in showers.

As though thinking about him made him appear, in walked Malik with Jacob and Tyler. I dipped my head to my journal again, not wanting to meet his gaze. I was terrified he'd take one look at me and *know* I'd been the person who'd popped his shower door open this morning. I remembered his startled yelp, and snuck a glance. He seemed okay. He was joking and making Tyler laugh. No sign of his hoodie, either.

So maybe he wasn't freaked out about a disappearing shower prowler.

I straightened in my chair. Mr. Jones was going to find out who Beardy McBeardface was, and Malik had no idea I'd nearly seen him ready for his morning shower.

Maybe today wasn't going to be a total disaster after all.

❖

"Did you hear?" Grayson said. "Total disaster."

"I didn't hear anything. I just got here," I said, sliding my backpack off one shoulder. "Which you just saw happen."

He'd come up to me the moment I'd gotten through the door—which had tried to pull at me, and through which I could feel the popping sensation again—and started talking at me.

"No hot guy," he said. "There will be *no hot guy.*"

"Wait. What?" I looked past him and saw Lindsey and Rhonda talking with Nat. Even Alec was here. They were putting the seats in a circle. I looked back at him. "You lost me."

"Kanata isn't joining us," Nat said. "For the party."

"Oh," I said. Then, after a second, "*Oh.*" I looked at Grayson. Hot Kanata Guy wasn't coming to our party. I suppose that qualified as a disaster in some warped sense of the word. "Got it." Then I frowned. "Why not?"

"They've got plans," Nat said, speaking a little louder than they usually did. "And it's not a disaster. It's just unfortunate."

"We'll still have pretty much the same number of people as last year," Lindsey said. "Central is coming."

"And they love the idea of Meeples. Everyone did. Everyone else is coming."

Grayson threw himself down on a chair. "Fine. It still sucks, though."

I had to fight off a smile. To my surprise, I saw Alec was doing the same thing. It was great to see him here.

"What are they doing instead?" I asked, curious.

Nat shrugged. "I don't know. I didn't ask, and Trish didn't say." They looked uncomfortable, and it struck me there might be more to this than Nat was letting on. I gave them a little frown, but they shook their head. Okay. Later, maybe.

I wasn't used to seeing Nat even a little bit rattled.

"I guess we can start," they said, and the rest of us sat down.

Minutes didn't take long, and although I paid attention and was interested, it struck me that it felt like someone was missing. I glanced at Alec and was happy to see him there. I wasn't missing him.

I wished Malik was here.

Well. I couldn't do anything about that. And this was our second-last official meeting.

I shook it off and listened as Nat brought us all up to speed.

"Candice wanted to host it for free," they said.

"Because she's awesome," I said.

"But I told her we'd absolutely pay what we could. And I sent a copy of her menu through to the other clubs so they know what to expect." Nat shrugged. "And that's really all I've got."

The group broke into little conversations. I turned to Grayson. "Hey, remember that substitute?"

He blinked. "Huh?"

"The teacher with the beard. Out by the trees?"

"Oh, sure."

"Did you have him for any classes?"

Grayson shook his head.

I took a breath and turned back to the group at large. Lindsey was leaning on Rhonda. Nat was talking with them, and Alec was checking something on his phone.

"Did anyone have a sub last week?" I said, loud enough to interrupt.

They all turned and looked at me. Alec shook his head. Lindsey and Rhonda said no. Nat shook their head, too.

"Did any of you see him?" I pulled out my phone. I pulled up the picture of Beardy McBeardface and held it out. Everyone came and looked.

"Yeah, that's him," Grayson said. "From the field. But I didn't have any classes with him or anything."

"What's wrong?" Alec said, staring at me.

"Probably nothing. Mr. Jones is on it. I just wondered. I caught him kind of staring at me. A couple of times."

"Gross," Grayson said, looking at the picture. "Now, if Mr. Jones was doing the staring..."

"It would *also* be gross," Nat said. "He's a little old for you. And married." They nudged Grayson's shoulder and took a second look at my phone. They looked back at me. "Staring?"

I shook my head and repeated myself. "It's probably nothing." Except now I didn't believe it.

"He did stare," Grayson said. "I remember."

"It happened a few times," I said. "In the hallway." I nodded to the music room door. "He was right…"

The music room door.

"…there." My voice went flat.

The music room door. The doors to the field. Outside Meeples. Everywhere I'd seen Beardy McBeardface…

"Cole?" Alec touched my shoulder, interrupting my train of thought.

"It's probably nothing," I said again. Third time's the charm. Except…All the places I'd seen the man were places I'd teleported. Doors I'd used.

So, probably not nothing.

Probably a disaster after all.

To-Do

- Bearded rando. Sub? Talk to principal?

Cole the Teenage Freak

- ~~Concentrate at doors. All the doors. Every time. You got this!~~
- ☐ Locked doors. One way?
- Blood sugar? Hungry? Definitely hungry.
- ☐ CARRY YOUR PHONE.
- ☐ Doors. Again. <u>You don't got this</u>. EVEN THE SHOWER.
- ☐ No door required for exit?
- ☐ Pull getting stronger. Bad? ~~Good?~~
- ☐ Popping thing. Like fireworks.
- ☐ Places I've never been!
- ☐ Beardy McBeardface can tell?
- ☐ Stop practicing. Just stop doing it at all.

SIXTEEN

I was determined to make it through the day without any accidental teleportation adventures, but the day was conspiring against me, including a typical Tozer family morning of complete snooze-button abuse which led to missing my bus and barely making it to school on time via a begged ride from my dad.

Even at a half run, every single time I went through a door—*especially* my own shower—I managed to stay put. It took effort. The doors *wanted* me to take a trip. The pull was a little bit stronger every time, and I caught myself trying to plan my day around going through as few doors as possible.

This was a futile plan in a world full of buildings. For example? Bedroom door. Bathroom door. Shower door, twice. Bathroom door again. Front door. Both sets of double doors at school. The door to homeroom.

And that was just before classes started.

Mr. Jones took me aside in the morning after homeroom to tell me there hadn't been a substitute teacher last week and to tell him or any teacher if I saw the man again and he made me feel at all uncomfortable. He thought it was likely the man was a parent, and said none of the other teachers and no one in the office had seen anyone unusual otherwise. He repeated that he was taking me seriously so many times my skin started to itch with wanting to get out of the classroom. Thankfully, the bell rang, and I had to go.

I did consider the photos I had on my phone but decided not to show him. If this *was* about my teleportation problem, did I really want to get Mr. Jones involved? I wasn't sure it was a great idea. I liked Mr. Jones, but I wasn't sure liking him was enough to tell him I could teleport and trust he wouldn't have me committed.

By the time my morning classes were done (four more doors total, in and out), and I hadn't teleported anywhere or seen Beardy McBeardface, I'd decided I was maybe overreacting. We were doing review, too, and I made it through both classes without feeling like I hadn't learned anything all year, which was another solid entry in the plusses side of things.

I even got both derivative questions right in Calculus.

It was raining, so I had lunch at our usual table (cafeteria line doors, in and out). I tried to get involved with the conversation Nat was having with Alec about a sci-fi show they both watched on Netflix, but I hadn't seen most of it, and so I just sat back and kind of enjoyed seeing Alec back with the group.

Two more classes (four more trips through doorways) and it was time to grab my stuff from my locker (two doors on either end of the stairwell) and head home. Pushing through the front doors of the school, I grunted with the effort of staying put. A couple of kids turned and stared. It was a really loud grunt because so much pull hooked into the center of my chest.

When I made it through the doors, the snapping sensation of moving past was so sudden I nearly tripped.

Definitely getting stronger.

I took a second to stand under the awning. My bus wasn't here. I leaned against the brick wall as other students streamed out of the building. Some were going to the student parking, usually in groups. Some were heading to where the buses lined up, one bus already there. And some hovered like I was, finding spots out of the rain to wait.

My phone buzzed. I checked it. Sportsball.

Is this year done yet?

Only half a week left, I wrote. *And then exams.*

Don't remind me.

I smiled. I glanced around, but I didn't see him anywhere. *You'll ace them*, I sent.

He sent me an emoji with its eyebrow raised. Seriously? I caught myself grinning and was looking through the emojis for something to send back when he texted again.

You sure about that?

I stopped scrolling and went back to the alphabet.

I'll put it on my list. Sportsball gets all A's.

What if I don't?

Then I'll never get to fill in the little box. It'll be on my list forever.

Too much pressure.

I laughed, glancing up. My bus was finally pulling in. By the time I got in and sat down, he'd sent another message.

You studying at Meeples again?

I am tomorrow, I wrote, deciding so at that very moment. I hit Send, and then I hesitated just a few seconds before adding: *you in?* Everything Candice had said replayed in my head while the bus pulled out. I held my breath.

Sure. Same time?

I sent him a thumbs-up and tried not to grin.

I failed.

By the time I got home, I was ridiculously upbeat. The front door didn't fight me too much, and my dad took one look at me and signed, *you had good day!* It wasn't a question.

I did, I signed. *You?*

He told me about his clients, and then we cleaned up the general mayhem from breakfast that morning before we started working on dinner. Dad was in a good mood, too, and he decided instead of a stir fry, we'd have a salad and chicken breasts and roasted potatoes, which is normally a Sunday night thing. I wasn't going to argue, even if I was relegated to peeling potatoes. Dad's potatoes were worth it. By the time my mom got home, dinner was almost ready and I was setting the dining room table, which we almost never used.

"What's the special occasion?" she asked.

"No reason."

Dad came in and dropped off the salad. *He has been grinning since he got home.* He went back to the kitchen. He was *such* a traitor.

"I just had a good day, that's all."

She used her mom-vision, and I tried not to squirm. "Any details you'd like to share?"

I shrugged. "It was just a good day." For example, I didn't end up teleporting into anyone's bathroom.

Dad returned with plates and we all sat down.

Hey, I signed. *It okay if I go study at Meeples tomorrow? After school. Back for dinner.*

They exchanged a quick glance, doing their parent telepathy thing before my dad agreed it would be fine.

"On your own or with a *friend*?" my mother asked and signed.

"A friend," I said and signed right back. "Meeples is a great place to study."

"Ah," she said. Something in the way she said it made me look up at her, and her smile went right to her eyes. Uh-oh. *Dita Wallace's daughter?* I swear she took joy in fingerspelling the name like that.

I swallowed some salad. *Son. Yes.*

"Ah," she said again. Her tone rose a little bit higher.

"I need water," I said and signed, getting up from the table and heading into the kitchen. I poured a glass of water and tried to force the blush I knew was spreading up my neck to go away. I could hear them both chuckling in the dining room.

Parents are the worst.

To-Do

- ■ Bearded rando. Sub? Talk to principal?
- ☐ Rework speech for Rainbow Club
- ☐ Meeples with Sportsball

Cole the Teenage Freak

- ■ ~~Concentrate at doors. All the doors. Every time. You got this!~~
- ☐ Locked doors. One way?
- ■ Blood sugar? Hungry? Definitely hungry.
- ☐ CARRY YOUR PHONE.
- ☐ Doors. Again. <u>You don't got this</u>. EVEN THE SHOWER.
- ☐ No door required for exit?
- ☐ Pull getting stronger. Bad? ~~Good?~~
- ☐ Popping thing. Like fireworks.
- ☐ Places I've never been!
- ☐ Beardy McBeardface can tell?
- ☐ Stop practicing. Just stop doing it at all.

SEVENTEEN

It wasn't until I sat down for the final official meeting of our Rainbow Club that it really, really hit me. This was it. Next week exams, and then...

Well, then summer. Fine. We'd all be around for summer.

But *after* summer?

It would be over. High school.

I'd been planning on that moment for...well, forever. And now?

I looked around the room. This year there had mostly been the six of us. Me, Nat, Lindsey, Rhonda, Grayson, and Alec, and for a lot of this year, no Alec. Grayson and Nat would still be here next year, but I didn't know if the club could make it with just two members. Then again, we'd only had four last year before Lindsey and Rhonda had joined.

Nat caught me looking at them and tilted their head.

"Just wondering what you'll do next year," I said.

They smiled. "I have plans. Mr. Jones said he'll help make sure the club gets noise for all the new grade nines."

"It's going to be weird not seeing you people," I said a little louder.

"Don't you dare," Lindsey said, raising one finger at me from across the circle of chairs. "No crying. We've got the party after exams. Save it for then."

"Fine, fine."

Nat read through the minutes, and then we went over the specifics about our party at Meeples. The other schools were carpooling, since it was technically going to be after the school year, and we'd get there first to help Candice set a few things up.

"You're still good to do an end-of-the-year speech?" Nat said.

"Yeah," I said, opening my bullet journal and reminding myself to go over the speech again.

And then, just like that, we were done.

"And that," Nat said, with a little smile, "is the queer agenda for the year."

"Ten percent is not enough, recruit, recruit, recruit!" Grayson chanted.

The rest of us applauded.

After that, we sat around talking, and I pulled out my phone to get a couple of shots so I could sketch them later. Alec and Rhonda listening to Lindsey. Grayson laughing and Nat trying hard not to give in and laugh at whatever inappropriate thing he'd just said. Then I stopped being a wallflower and joined in. Lindsey was deciding what games we should focus on, and I was all about making sure they weren't all Settlers of Catan, because I might be okay with losing nonstop to her, but we should at least let some of the guests from other schools win something.

It went on like that for a while, and then it was done. No one seemed to want to be the first person to go. Lindsey and Rhonda had stood up, which had made us all get up and get ready, but we were all hesitating again.

I went over to Nat, catching them alone. "So, can I ask what happened with Kanata now?"

They blinked, and a little flush crept up their cheeks. They glanced around, but no one was watching us.

"Their leader and I got in a bit of a thing last Pride," Nat said. "I think she decided they were busy because of that."

"A thing?" I lowered my voice. I tried to remember back to the summer, and I did kind-of-sort-of remember something. "The 'Love Is Love' thing, right?"

Nat nodded. "I mentioned it wasn't particularly trans or ace inclusive, and she got upset."

"Wow," I said. "And she got mad?"

"*Really* mad. Like, 'I was attacking her in public' mad."

"I'm sorry," I said. "Why didn't you tell us?"

Nat took a second to think. To be honest, I loved that about them. They seemed to be capable of organizing their thoughts in all these levels that I didn't have access to. It would have been intimidating if they weren't so freaking willing to teach all the time.

Lindsey and Rhonda waved, finally breaking the invisible seal of the room. We waved back.

"You need a ride?" Alec asked me.

"No," I said. "I'm good."

"Could you drop me off?" Grayson asked him.

Both Nat and I tensed, but Alec just nodded. "Sure."

They left together.

"Okay," I said. "That just happened."

"I'm glad." Nat said. "I know Grayson wanted to apologize, and I don't know if he already did or not. If he didn't, I'm guessing he's about to."

"Wow," I said.

"It felt like I screwed up," Nat said.

It took me a second to reconnect what they'd said with our previous conversation. The 'Love Is Love' Pride thing. *"You?* But she's the one who didn't clue in."

Nat shrugged. "I know. But at the time…" They exhaled. "You all kind of look at me like I've got all the answers."

"Because you usually do."

Nat blushed again. "Thank you. But I don't. I could have sent her a private message. I was just super tired. Like, Pride was so exhausting. It's supposed to be this day where I get to be *me*, but so much didn't include me. And her post was the final straw on a bad day. I kind of blew the delivery. My friend Talia said I hit her with a clue-by-four."

We laughed, but I could see they were sort of forcing it.

"New agenda item," I said.

They looked at me.

"This year, when Pride comes around, I'll start a group message with all of us. If stuff happens, we'll handle it as a group. That way it doesn't have to be you doing all the speaking all the time. It's not fair."

"That would be nice," Nat said.

"Besides," I said, "imagine how much better it would have gone if Grayson had handled it."

They laughed, a surprised, loud sound that sort of escaped them without any warning.

"I'm totally getting better at this joke thing," I said.

They swatted me.

When the door opened, I was almost not surprised to see Malik. He smiled, just a little bit awkwardly. "Sorry, am I early?"

"No," Nat said. "We were done." They glanced at me, and with their back to Malik, one eyebrow crept up. *Seriously.* It was an epidemic. "I'll see you at the party."

"See you," I said.

They left, and Malik offered up another smile as they passed.

I picked up my bag. "Everyone was a bit sad," I said. "No one wanted to be the first to leave."

"Ah," he said. He looked around the music room for a second.

I pulled out my phone. "I'm just going to remind my parents we're heading to Meeples and then we can go. I don't need them forgetting and blowing up my phone."

"Okay," he said. Did he sound nervous? That was dumb. Why would he be nervous?

But I felt a little jolt of nerves in my stomach as I typed out the text. That didn't make sense. I mean, we were going to hang out and study at Meeples. It wasn't like it was a date.

❖

By the time we got to Meeples, the sky had gotten a bit grim. We ducked inside just in time to see the first of the rain come down behind us. Candice waved us in, and we waited for her at the counter as she finished serving her tables.

"Hello again," she said to Malik once she was free.

"Hi," Malik said.

"Back for more study time?" Her smile was genuine, but I wanted to head off the sparkle in her eyes fast.

"Yep. I'm down for a mocha and a lemon square," I said, turning to Malik.

"Me too," he said.

Once Candice cut the squares, we took them and found our own table. We sat, and I avoided glancing at Malik. It was stupid, but I couldn't stop myself. I stared at my bag, pulled out my books as though they'd vanish if I didn't keep my eyes on them at all times, and even checked my phone, putting it on the table beside my notes. I took a bite of my lemon square and studied the plate like it would be on my exams.

"Here you go," Candice said. She put down our mochas and gave me another sparkly eyed smile before she walked off.

"She's really nice," Malik said.

I glanced at him. Had his skin always had that bronze undertone? He looked…warm. I was pretty sure my own face was blazing red.

"I'm a fan," I said, and then I winced, because who says that about middle-aged women who run geeky bookstore gaming cafés? Well, other than me. Without really thinking about it, I started fingerspelling. *Geek. Nerd. Game.*

"What does that mean?" Malik said.

My hand froze. "Oh. I'm fingerspelling."

He smiled. "I've seen you do that before."

He had? Oh God. "It's a nervous habit," I said, and then I wished I hadn't because—

"You're nervous?"

—because *that.*

I blew out a breath. "Kind of?"

He just waited, looking at me. Big brown eyes. Patient smile. If he did the one-eyebrow thing right now, I'd probably fall off my chair. Thankfully, he didn't.

"Maybe more anxious than nervous," I said, hedging a bit. "I've been kind of procrastinating a lot lately." Okay, that wasn't hedging. It was outright lying. Teleporting all over the place, weird bearded men following me…That didn't really fall under "procrastination." But it did cut into my study plans.

"I hear that," Malik said, taking a bite of his lemon square. I tried not to stare at his mouth. My fingers moved. *Mouth.*

"You're doing it again."

"I am."

"How was the club?"

He changed the conversation, almost like he was being kind or something. I was happy to accept it, though. "Weird. Sad. But good."

And there was the eyebrow. I focused on staying upright in my chair. "Sad?"

"Last one," I said. "I mean, not really. I'll see everyone at the end-of-the-year party, but it was the last official meeting. I know I have all summer, too, but…" I shrugged. "But that was it."

"It was like that with the last game, too," he said.

I smiled. I liked the analogy. "I guess they are kind of my team, right?" Then I chuckled. "Though the thought of us all trying to do something coordinated and sportsball-like is unlikely."

"I sure wouldn't want to face off against Alec," Malik said.

"He's a teddy bear," I said. It just popped right out. I held up one finger. "You cannot tell him I ever said that."

Malik laughed. "I promise."

The weird whatever-it-was had faded. I exhaled again and opened my books. Malik did the same, and we got down to some serious study time. I stared at the math and felt a deep, bone-numbing boredom settle in even before I'd gotten through a single page of my notes. There was just nothing enjoyable about calculus.

Even when you had the cutest guy in school sitting across from you.

We were on our second mochas when my phone pinged, and I saw the text from my mother.

It's pouring down. Do you and your friend need a ride home?

I glanced out the window. Mom was right. Rain was sheeting outside.

"My mom's offering a ride home," I said.

Malik hesitated, looked at the rain, then nodded. "Okay. That'd be great."

I tapped out a reply on my phone. *Okay. Please do not embarrass me or him.*

Jann Arden sing-along it is, she sent back. *On my way.* She must have been late leaving work again.

"Fair warning," I said. "My mom has mom-taste in music."

Malik smiled.

❖

It turned out to be a bluff. No music was playing when we threw ourselves into Mom's car, dashing out when we saw her pull up in front of Meeples. I took the back seat so Malik could give her directions to his place.

"Mom, this is Malik. Malik, this is my mom." I worked hard to put the right amount of *this is no big deal, Mother, please do not make this a big deal* into my voice.

"Call me Jennifer," my mom said. "It's nice to meet you."

"Hi." Malik bobbed his head. "Thank you for the ride." Man, he was polite. She was going to eat that up.

"It's no trouble," she said, but I could tell she'd really liked that he'd thanked her. "Where am I headed?"

Malik gave her his address and told her the best way to get there, and she pulled back out into traffic.

After a moment, she glanced at him. "So, Cole says your mother is an author?"

Malik nodded. "She uses a pen name. Dita Wallace."

"I've read her." She met my gaze in the rearview. "She's really good."

"I'll tell her," Malik said. "Thank you."

Okay, this wasn't so bad.

"So," my mother said, and I held my breath. "What are your plans after graduation?"

And here it came. I tried to catch my mother's eyes in the rearview again, but she avoided me, smiling and glancing at Malik.

"Uh," he said. "I might be taking a gap year."

Really? I hadn't known that.

"Oh?" My mom said. It didn't come out judgy or anything—thank God—just interested.

"I have a couple of ideas, I just don't know which one to do. I applied everywhere. College, to U of T, and Ottawa, and Carleton. My uncle offered me a job with his crew," Malik said. "He's a contractor, and an electrician. They do renovations and stuff. For the summer at least. It's just gopher work. I won't get to do a lot of construction stuff, but I can stay with him and figure out if it's what I want to do. If I do, then I'll go to school in September. If I don't..." He bit his bottom lip. "I can defer. My mom says it's just as important to figure out what you *don't* want to do."

"That's smart," my mother said, and now she made eye contact with me again. Pointed eye contact. What was happening? "I did most of a psychology degree before I figured out I didn't want to be a psychiatrist."

"Yeah," Malik said. "It's a lot of money and time and..." He shrugged, like he was embarrassed to admit it. "I don't really know what I want to do."

"What was the other idea?"

Okay, enough was enough. "I feel like I should have warned you," I said, leaning forward. "My mother interrogates all my friends."

My mother rolled her eyes, but Malik laughed. "No, it's cool. The other idea is the military."

Whoa. I blinked. "Really?"

EIGHTEEN

The last day of school was blurring by. My teachers seemed as ready for it to be over as we were, and although they paid lip service to exam prep and review, suddenly it was lunch.

I was the last one to the table because of the usual lineup at the cafeteria, thankfully, and not because of any accidental jumps home via the swinging doors. Alec bumped shoulders with me when he caught me sort of *staring* at everyone.

"Don't get all weird," he said.

"Way too late," Grayson said.

"Years," Lindsey agreed.

I gasped at her, hand over my heart. "Et tu, Lindsé?"

She just grinned.

We ate and laughed and talked, and though maybe I glanced around the cafeteria a few times to see if I could find a certain sportsball guy, I was pretty much the happiest I'd ever been at this school. It figured it would take me to the last possible day to get it right.

I opened my journal and did a super-fast sketch of the group of us, almost cartoonish. It wasn't my usual style, but it was fun. By the time I was done, Nat was leaning over and watching me work.

"You're really good at that."

"Only when I have something to look at," I said. I glanced at them. They had the coolest bow tie on today. The bow was made of wood, and the cloth that tied it in place was a super-bright fuchsia. "Have I ever told you I love your bow ties?"

They smiled. "No."

"Well, I do."

Their pale skin pinked, right to the tips of their ears.

"Nat is right. You should do a cartoon," Rhonda said.

I looked up. "A cartoon?"

"Yeah, like, all of us," Grayson said. "You could make us into superheroes or something. The Gayvengers."

"Never listen to him," Lindsey said. "But she's right. You could do a cartoon."

"Like Sophie Labelle," Nat said.

"I'm not *that* good, guys." But the thing was, I kind of liked the idea.

"Oh come on," Grayson said. "The thought of something you need to practice makes your heart go pitter-pat." He leaned across the table. "I should be the hero, though. I mean, look at my hair." He tapped my drawing. "That hair says 'hero.'"

"Is *that* what it's saying?" Alec said. "Huh. That's totally not what I thought it was saying."

Grayson shoved him, and Alec shoved him back. They were totally cool with each other. I glanced at Nat, and they gave me one of their little smiles. They'd caught it, too.

"Maybe," I said. But I could tell they'd all seen right through me. I was totally going to try. I could start a new Tumblr, maybe. I could do little scenes from our Rainbow Club, maybe. In a way, I could hold on to them a little longer.

When lunch ended, I walked with Alec to his locker.

"So," I said. "You and Grayson made up? He apologized?"

"Yeah."

I blinked. "'Yeah'? That's it? That's all I get? After suffering through a year of drama, of both of you melting down at the mention of each other's name, you're giving me 'yeah.'" I mimicked his grunty voice.

Alec closed his locker, spread his arms, and said, "Yeah."

"Jerk." Then I sighed. "I'm glad. I hated that you left the group. I shouldn't have let you. I shouldn't have let him make you feel like you weren't a part of it."

Alec looked at me for a couple of seconds before he smiled. "I know you have my back."

Oh man. I would not cry at school. Nope. *Wuss*, I fingerspelled.

"But I'll make you a deal," Alec said. "I'll tell you all about how Grayson groveled, if…" He drew out the word.

"If?" I said.

"If you tell me who you've been looking for all week, all the time." He crossed his arms. "Like I can't guess."

I shook my head. There was no way I was going to—

"Hey, Cole," Malik said. He was passing by with Tyler.

"Hey," I said. It came out all strained, and I had to clear my throat after. They were gone a moment later.

When I turned to look at Alec again, his mouth was doing the stupid wiggle thing it did when he was trying not to laugh.

"Not a word," I said.

Alec just patted my shoulder and went off to his class.

❖

"I'm home," I called out.

When I came in through the front door—concentrating on staying put, which was totally a habit now and I had this *not teleporting* thing down, *thankyouverymuch*—I dumped my bag, phone, and jacket and started working on my shoes.

My mom came through the kitchen. "Whoa," I said. "Check you out." She was wearing a light blue dress and the gold necklace my dad had gotten her for their fifteenth anniversary. I gave her a thumbs-up once I got my shoes off. "You look great."

"Thank you," she said. She'd even put her hair up.

"I'm guessing it's a fancier Date Night tonight?"

"We're going to the Inn to have an early dinner with the Websters, and then we've got the theatre."

My father stepped into the kitchen. He had on his black jacket, a black shirt, and a tie I was pretty sure was the same blue as my mother's dress. They were like that. It was cringeworthy embarrassing, but they liked to match for Date Night activities.

He hugged her from behind and kissed the small of her neck.

"You are both doing serious emotional damage to your offspring," I said and signed.

He let go of her. *Parental obligation*, he signed. *Pizza money.* He pointed to the kitchen counter.

I forgive, I signed.

They both laughed.

How your last day go?

"Honestly?" I said and signed. "It was *amazing*. My friends are great. I'm great." The weird freaks who were following me are gone. "I don't know what it is, but…" I shrugged. "I'll take it."

My dad patted my back as they passed me, and my mom gave me

a kiss on the cheek, and then they were heading out the front door. I followed them, waiting until they got into the car and pulled out of the driveway before I waved.

My folks would be out late. I had pizza money. Candice seemed to think Malik King had maybe been checking me out, and Alec seemed to agree. Alec and Grayson had made up. And the biggest plus on the list? There'd been no sign of Beardy McBeardface in a couple of days, and even though I could feel the door behind me pulling at me, I hadn't teleported anywhere in a couple of days.

All things told? I was having the best day of my life.

So, y'know, of course that's when someone grabbed me from behind and yanked me through my front door.

Poof.

NINETEEN

The tug-snap felt different. It jarred and yanked and shoved rather than the flow I was used to. I had just enough time to notice the sensation of teleporting against my will was meaner somehow before my instincts kicked in.

The single most important thing you learn in self-defense classes is not about hurting anyone. It's not about fighting anyone, either. It's about *avoiding* getting hurt in the first place. Ideally? You never touch anyone. You learn how to scope out trouble, you avoid the trouble, and you keep those around you from getting hurt, too. That's always goal one.

But, having been grabbed from behind, I was skipping past that and aiming for the next best thing: getting away.

Whoever it was had one hand over my mouth, the other grabbing my arm. I could either work against their sense of balance, though I didn't have a clear picture of how they were standing—or cause them pain and run like hell.

I opted for number two without thinking about it too hard. I'm not sure what that might have said about me as a person, but y'know, I was in the moment.

I elbowed back hard with my free arm, stomped on their foot, and bit their hand. Maybe not in that order. It was kind of quick and messy, and I was running on instincts I'd learned in the self-defense class by practicing over and over again.

The noises of pain my attacker made were really, really satisfying. They let go. I dove ahead to get out of the attacker's grasp, but a quick glance around told me *ahead* wasn't going to cut it. I was in a room. My brain didn't land on any particulars at all except it was a fairly small room without a door I could see. I whirled on my feet just in time to see my attacker stepping back through one and closing it. He was a redhead, and he was wheezing, and I had one tiny moment of triumph before I realized he was closing the only damn door behind him.

"No!" I dove for it, but I heard the click before I got to the door. Also, my side didn't have a handle.

Well, shit.

I tried to get a grip on it anyway, but all I could do was make it wiggle a tiny bit. Definitely locked.

Fuck. I pressed my hand against the surface.

Fuck fuck fuck.

❖

When he didn't come back right away, I took a second to take stock. I didn't have my phone, so calling for help with a handy GPS device wasn't going to work. I eyed the door, wondering if I could maybe get through it and teleport faster than they could stop me when they opened it to come back in. It was a possibility. I had no idea if it was a good possibility.

Other than that? This place was obviously a small room repurposed as a jail cell. The thought was not calming in the slightest. A small cot with a single sheet was against one wall, but when I tried to lift it, it wouldn't budge off the floor. I checked. It was bolted into the tiles.

Well, that wasn't disturbing at all.

There was a small sink, no plug or chain, and beside that, a toilet. A recessed light was in the ceiling, but I didn't see a switch. Probably outside the door.

I started to finger-spell. *Door. Cot. Toilet.*

It didn't calm me down.

A little window provided a small amount of light. Maybe I could—

I heard a sound at the door, and I tensed. I wasn't sure my idea of rushing the door was a good one, but I didn't really have another option. I braced myself.

When the door opened though, three men were standing there, and it was clear I wouldn't be running anywhere. They were bigger than me, and the door opened *into* the room. They took up all the space the room had to offer.

I backed up, despite myself.

I recognized Beardy McBeardface from school. Substitute teacher, my ass. He was standing in the middle of the three men, looking like he was more or less in charge of whatever this was. To his right was a guy who looked somewhat familiar. He was an older guy, kind of *stiff* looking. He had a suit and tie, and for some reason I thought they weren't the right colors. It clicked. The guy from Meeples, who'd come in after I'd teleported there after Malik had first come to the Rainbow Club. The one that had stared at me and Alec.

Holy crap. Had these guys been following me for the last *two weeks*?

To Beardy's left was a shorter man, not as old as Beardy. He had red hair and freckles, and was glaring at me. I wondered if this was my attacker. I hadn't really gotten a good look at him before, what with the elbows and biting and the slammed door, but then he closed his right hand around a bandage. Yep. I'd totally bitten Freckle-Face.

"What do you want?" I'd intended a strong voice, showing no fear, but it maybe came out a bit whiny, and I had to clear my throat.

"I'm genuinely sorry this is how we had to meet," Beardy said. He had a nice, calm voice. He spoke like we were chatting in a café or something. His smile seemed totally genuine behind the beard, and a small, basic part of me wondered if I should just maybe listen to what he had to say. Then I remembered I'd been kidnapped and spied on.

"Let me go," I said. That came out stronger.

Beardy held up his hands as if to tell me not to bite him, and then he took one more step into the room.

I retreated the same amount. One more step, and I'd be back against the wall by the cot.

"I'm not going to hurt you, Cole," he said.

"How do you know my name?"

He exhaled. "I need to know if you told anyone."

I blinked. Told them *what*? Then I blinked again. Oh. Of course. These guys had grabbed me and teleported me here, so obviously they were all teleporty types, which meant Beardy McBeardface was asking me if I'd told anyone I could teleport.

I hesitated. Was any answer right? If I told him yes, was that like being in a movie and saying if I wasn't at home by the right time, some sort of document would be leaked to the press? Or was a "yes" just adding a new name to the list of people to kidnap?

"Good," Beardy said, like I'd already answered.

Damn. I really sucked at this stuff.

I swallowed. "What are you going to do to me? People will care if I just disappear." This was totally true. I mean, it didn't help me if they killed me and dumped me in a hole somewhere, but people would definitely care about it. Hell, this is one time Colenap would work in my favor. I'd already been kidnapped once. If I vanished again? That'd be major news.

"We're not going to hurt you," Beardy said again. Even with the smile and the raised hands, I totally didn't believe him. My dad had taught me people said as much with their eyes as they did with their mouths and their hands. The hands said, "Hey, I'm no threat." The mouth said, "Totally on your side." The eyes?

The eyes were saying, "I need to get this over with."

"You're too young," he said, as if I'd asked him a question. I suppose I had, but I wasn't sure what my age had to do with anything.

"Come again?"

"It takes an adult with a level head to have what we have and be responsible," Beardy said. "And most of us don't gain the aptitude until we're in our twenties. I've no doubt you'll be an excellent addition to our institution, Cole, but…not yet."

Aptitude? Institution?

"How many of you are there?"

"There's no point in going over the details right now, Cole. We need to relock your gift again."

"Again?"

He twitched and then shook his head. "It'll be easier if you don't resist. We can do more than open doorways, Cole. We can close things, too."

Okay, whatever *that* meant? It sounded totally like something I should resist.

"You?" I said. "Are creepy as fuck. Let me out of here, right now, or I will scream as loud as I can."

"No one to hear you," Freckle-Face said, and he sounded really happy about that. I decided that if I ever had the chance, I was going to bite him again.

Beardy aimed a quick frown at Freckle-Face, who didn't seem to care much. Mr. Stiff just looked bored.

"I am sorry," Beardy said. "But the good news is you won't remember any of this."

"Wha—?" I started to say, and then something awful wrapped itself around my head and set it on fire.

❖

Beardy McBeardface was trying to melt my brain.

Okay, that might not be *actually* what he was trying to do, but it sure felt like it. This kind of pressure suddenly appeared, but it was all in my head, like the world's worst headache decided to hook up with all the worst memories I'd ever had and then went dancing through my brain swinging flamethrowers.

I was at the museum, just like when this whole insane teleporting thing had started, but the whole place was on fire.

Then I was trapped in my locker, but my lungs were filling with smoke.

Now I was at Meeples, and flames licked up the sides of the bookshelves.

My old house.

My bedroom.

Through the haze of pain and fear, a distant part of me knew none of this had ever happened, but it felt like Beardy was somehow *making* me believe it did. And it was terrifying. I never wanted to think about it ever again.

I saw bodies and heard screams, and in every case, I was one of the people on fire, wailing in an agony of pain and trying to get out, but there was no way out...

This didn't happen.

I was standing under the Lancaster Bomber, the rest of the planes in the large museum spread out around me, fire leaping up the walls and moving from exhibit to exhibit.

And Beardy was with me. I could feel him, like he was right behind me. His presence had that same tug-and-snap feeling to it, like if I just knew where to look, I could yank and pull him here...

I ignored the flames, telling myself over and over they didn't exist. It wasn't real. This was like some sort of nightmare, and nightmares weren't real.

Stop fighting.

Beardy's voice was creepy as fuck.

Go to hell.

I spoke without words, but I knew he could hear me.

With a loud crash, one of the planes fell from the ceiling into the raging fires that had spread beneath them. Coughing, I crouched lower. There was no way out. I was surrounded by fire, and people were screaming, though I couldn't see them. People were dying. It was horrifying.

You won't remember this. You will bury it as a traumatic memory, and you won't have to see me again. Not until you're ready. Stop fighting me, Cole.

It wasn't real. None of this was real. I coughed and coughed. I couldn't breathe. I was going to die in the freaking aviation museum and…

Everything started to go a little blurry around the edges.

That's right. Beardy's voice was so soft and gentle, and so damn friendly.

I remembered his eyes, though.

Hey, asshole, I said, again without words. If there was an equivalent to shouting in whatever it was we were doing, I was aiming for the higher range of decibels. *You're a freak. This. Isn't. Real!* I grabbed on to the little tug I could feel whenever he "spoke" and pulled it as hard as I could.

I heard Beardy cry out in surprise, and then I turned to see the front glass entranceway of the museum explode as a huge wave of water blasted through the doors. It blew past me, and for just a moment when it hit me, I could have sworn I heard Beardy swear.

Then I was gone.

❖

Someone—no, someones—were holding me underwater, and I was running out of air. I could see the sunlight hitting the water and the dark shadows their forms cast as they held me down. I twisted and fought, bubbles moving past my mouth as I screamed.

I could hear the people holding me, above the surface of the water, saying, "Just forget it, just forget it!"

Water was filling my mouth. I was going to die.

I pushed hard against the ground beneath me—a lake, maybe, or a pond. It gave way a little, but I threw everything I had into it, and their grips slipped.

I struggled back to the surface and gasped for air.

And woke up.

I almost fell out of the cot-like bed in the awful little room. I was panting, gasping for breath as though I really had been underwater, and it took me more than a few seconds to get my breathing back under control.

Okay, whatever Beardy McBeardface just tried to do to me was not something I was willing to try again. I felt wobbly and weak, and I was pretty sure next time they would bring someone more capable at whatever brain-melty thing they were trying to do to me.

I liked my brain. It might be a nerdy, geeky, hyper-organized brain, but it was my freaking brain. I'd keep it unmelted, thanks.

I was rattled, but as far as I could tell, I remembered everything. I didn't feel like I had any gaping holes. Museum. Locker. Many embarrassing moments in public. Check. Pretty sure I had my whole collection of Cole Tozer's Greatest Hits. I wasn't sure how I'd managed that particular feat, but I'd take it. I wasn't up for round two, and I had a terrible feeling once they realized I was awake, it would begin.

So. New plan. Get the hell out of this fucking room.

Well, okay, that was the old plan, too, but now it had a star beside it. A brain-melty star.

I still had all the same damn tools I had before. A cot I couldn't move, one sheet, no pillow. A sink. A toilet. Really, it was pretty basic as jail cells went, only without bars and just the one small window and…

It was dark out.

Oh my God, I'd been out all afternoon. Had Date Night ended? My parents would flip out if I wasn't there when they got home. I patted my pockets, but I still didn't have a phone. Or my bag and my jacket.

Okay, night-time put one new thing in my arsenal.

Desperation.

I eyed the window again. I heard my grandmother's voice, talking about my father when he was my age, when his hearing had started failing. She'd been a champion for him, fighting tooth and nail for everything they needed. She'd also told him in no uncertain terms that life didn't hand him anything he couldn't handle. My father rolled his eyes whenever she started in on the story, even though I could tell he loved her for it. But that's not the part I was thinking of. I was remembering the end, when my grandmother would wax poetic about how my father turned something that made his life challenging into a career helping others.

"Whenever a door closes, somewhere a window opens."

I looked up at the tiny window. A grown man would never fit through that window.

Luckily, I happened to come in size small.

"If this works, you never get to complain about being short ever again," I said as I pulled the sheet off the bed. I'd never broken a window before. I hoped it was more or less like in the movies. But when I managed to pull myself up to look out the window, I had a new problem.

Wherever I was, I was up high. Like, at least three stories. Maybe as much as five.

"Fuck." Okay. Okay. New plan…New plan… "Got anything else, Grandma?"

I stared at the damn window. I didn't have enough sheets. What good was a window instead of a door if I couldn't use it to get to the damn ground.

Wait.

Window instead of a door.

Could I do that?

What had Beardy McBeardface said? *We can do more than open doorways, Cole.*

I eyed the locked door. They could be here at any second. It wasn't like I had a whole lot of options. But the moment I broke the glass, I'd be in trouble. They'd hear it. And that meant maybe a minute or two. If it didn't work?

I bit my lip.

Well, worst case scenario, I could dangle outside a window, or maybe fall to my death, or…

"Not helping."

I wrapped the sheet around my fist. I was about to punch out a window and try teleporting to my bedroom.

Cole Tozer, Badass.

If life was a movie, Cole Tozer, Badass would have punched the glass out with one solid hit and flung himself through after pushing a few tiny pieces of leftover glass to the side.

In reality? It took me way more time than I'll ever admit, and my first punch did nothing but hurt my hand. Glass is tougher than it looks in the movies. I ended up putting my shoe on my hand and, after a few very pathetic attempts, I lost my temper and really whaled on the damn window, and it finally cracked.

After it cracked, it went a little faster. I was terrified the damn door would open behind me at any second, so I worked as fast as I could. Once it really broke, it sort of exploded into lots of tiny little pieces, and it didn't take much to wipe the frame clear of bits.

I put my shoe back on and took a few deep breaths. I was going to have to leap through the window. I wasn't going to have time to really stop, what with gravity and being very high off the ground and *whose idea was this anyway?*

Then I heard footsteps outside the door to my little cell, and that was it.

My bedroom. I focused as hard as I could. My bedroom window, specifically. It looked over my bed. The place where I slept. The place where I got to be me and no one judged. A safe place. The place where I had my first kiss with Brady, though really I didn't feel like replaying my kissing Brady much these days.

The door was opening.

I held on to the image as hard as I could, hauled myself up on the edge of the sill, and tipped out the window. I felt a tug, and I yanked it hard.

Poof.

TWENTY

I hit the floor hard, hands first, feeling the carpet burn my palms and wrists. It hurt, but I was no longer trapped in a tiny room by those suited freaks, so I was calling it a win, and—

Wait. *Carpet?* This wasn't my room. If I wasn't in my bedroom, where did I end up? More importantly, was I alone?

"What the hell?"

I knew that voice. A light clicked on. I looked up from the floor, and there, in his bed, which of course was in *his bedroom*, was Malik King.

Eyes wide and staring at me like I was about to attack him or something, Malik said, "Cole?"

"Hi," I said. Still lying on my stomach on his floor where I'd landed, I shifted myself up on my elbows. "Sorry."

He frowned, looking at me, and then at his window, and then back at me. "How did you—?"

"Malik?" A man's voice called through his bedroom door. "Are you okay?"

Malik's eyes widened, and he pointed to the side of the bed farthest from the bedroom door. I crab-crawled out of sight and dropped to the floor just as the door opened.

"Yeah, Dad, I'm okay."

"Did you drop something?"

"Nearly fell out of bed. Bad dream," Malik said. "Sorry. Didn't mean to wake you."

Malik was way better at making stuff up on the fly than I was. I should take notes.

"Okay," his father said. He had a nice voice. "You need anything?"

"No, I'm good." Malik paused. "Thanks."

A moment later, the door closed.

I exhaled and rolled onto my back.

Malik's head appeared over the edge of his bed. "What the *fuck*, Cole? What are you *doing* here?" He was whispering, but I could tell he wasn't happy. Which, okay, fair. Weird gay guy shows up in your bedroom after you come out to him? Not cool.

"Uh," I said. Mr. Eloquence.

He frowned. "How did you even get *up* here?"

It took me a second to realize what he meant. His bedroom was on the second floor of the house. I'd just dived in through his window. The King family didn't even have a convenient front yard tree to blame. I opened my mouth with no idea what I was going to say, when the reality of what had just happened struck me. Those people, those freaks, they'd been after me. They'd tried to do something to me. I'd just escaped being kidnapped—or worse.

I burst into tears.

So much for Cole Tozer, Badass.

We're not talking stoic movie hero tears, either. We're talking giant, body-shaking sobs that sounded more like burping hiccoughs and resulted in little bubbles of snot popping on my nose. I was in Malik King's bedroom after dark, and I was blubbering like I'd lost my mind.

"Whoa," Malik said, and then to my complete humiliation, he slid out of his bed and was hugging me on the floor. I shoved my face into the crook of my arm, trying to hold back, but my entire body was shaking.

"Hey, hey, Cole…" Malik said. "Are you okay? Do I need to call someone? What happened?" All the while, he ran one hand over my back in a small circle, pulling me against him with his other arm. It felt warm and safe, and I slowly got myself under control.

Also, Malik wasn't wearing a shirt, and Malik without a shirt was definitely a sight to behold. And here I was getting tears and spit and probably smearing snot all over him.

Fantastic.

"Sorry," I said again. My voice was rough. "I'm having a *really* bad night. Like, the *worst.*"

Malik let go and reached up behind him to his bedside table. He handed me a box of tissues. I used a couple to wipe my face.

"What happened?" he asked.

"I got snatched," I said. It just came out.

It felt so good to tell the truth. All my excuses: not worrying my parents, not wanting to look like I'd lost my mind, afraid people wouldn't believe me? They felt like the smallest things ever as soon as I told Malik. Why had I ever kept all this to myself?

"What?" His voice rose, and we both flinched. We waited a couple of seconds, but no one came to the door.

"I got grabbed. They took me somewhere, and—"

"Wait," he said. "Who? Who took you?"

"I don't really know. There are a few of them. I've seen them around a few times now, and they said they've been watching me. I thought one was a substitute teacher, and I think maybe one of them was at Meeples one time, but..." I shook my head as Malik's eyes widened. I sounded like I was insane. "I got away."

"And climbed up my house and through my window?"

"No," I said. I bit my lip. "No, that's not how I got here."

Malik frowned. I could practically see him deciding I was a lunatic. All those small doubts were back, and now they were huge doubts again. Man. A guy could get whiplash.

"You'd never believe me," I said.

"Try me."

I took a deep breath and used one last tissue to wipe the last of my meltdown off my face. How did I even start? The people who'd taken me were obviously like me: teleporters. Freckle-Face had grabbed me and yanked me through a door with him, and we'd ended up in that creepy-ass cell.

"There's something happening to me," I said. "And actually, it goes back to the locker thing."

I looked at Malik, and he nodded once. His dark eyes didn't leave mine. It was really distracting to have him looking at me like that, so I stared at the floor.

"It's going to sound crazy," I said. "I can't think of a way to say it that *isn't.*"

"Just say it," he said.

Please be cool. Please be cool. "I teleported."

Malik blinked. "What?"

"I can teleport. It keeps happening. I start to go through one door, and I end up coming out of a different door."

He scowled. "Cole," he started, voice low and annoyed.

"I dove though a window where the guy had taken me and came out through your window. I was aiming for my own bedroom. I guess I missed."

"You *missed.*" Malik crossed his arms.

"It's actually tougher than you think it is," I said, annoyed myself now. "I've only been at this for two weeks, and I can't always make it happen when I want to."

"Cole, it's the middle of the night, and I know I said I like you, but—"

"Oh God, no!" I said, holding up my hands. "I swear this isn't some stalker thing." Which, as soon as I said it, I realized was *totally* a thing a stalker would say. "This guy, I think he teleports too, he grabbed me and…" I trailed off. Malik was pushing himself back against his bed. In the small space on the floor between the wall and his bed, he had managed to get as far away from me as possible.

"You know what?" I said. "It doesn't matter. I need to go home. If I don't end up home before my parents, they'll totally flip. What time is it?"

I'd said all that in a rush. When Malik didn't answer, I looked around and saw he had an alarm clock beside his bed. It was nearly eleven. How late was their play? Were they doing anything after? My folks might already be home.

"I need to go. I need to…" I needed to figure out what the hell I was going to do about the teleporting freaks who were after me was what I needed to do. They weren't just tracking me. They were actively capable of popping in the same way I did. But I couldn't figure that out here. I got up.

"Cole," Malik said, rising. "You can't go downstairs. My parents. My dad is up."

"It's fine," I said. "I'll use your door."

"*What?*" His voice rose, and I could hear the unspoken "are you mental?" in his rough whisper.

"Seriously," I said, holding up both hands. "I'll be gone in a second. I'll teleport back to my place. I'm better with doors than windows." That wasn't exactly something I could say with complete certainty, but what the hell. So far it was true. I went to his bedroom door.

"Cole," Malik whispered again, sharp and annoyed. He obviously wasn't buying this whole "I can teleport" thing, but I was exhausted, I'd just been kidnapped, and frankly? I was totally past caring. Besides, he'd see soon enough. He couldn't deny it if I just vanished right in front of him.

I opened his door. "Seriously," I said. "It's fine."

I stepped through his bedroom door. I found the tug, thought of my bedroom...

Malik grabbed at my shoulder.

Poof.

Or, I guess, *poofs*.

Whoops.

TWENTY-ONE

Malik's jaw dropped. The open-mouth, no-words thing could have been really cute except his eyes were also wide open and he looked about ready to freak out. He was still holding on to my shoulder, which had shifted from a "wait, stop!" thing to a sort of a death grip now.

"Are you okay?" I said.

He stared at me. He hadn't blinked yet. That was probably bad, right? People needed to blink. And also breathe.

"Malik?" I said. "Can you please take a breath?"

"Where...?" He choked out the word, and then he sucked in a deep lungful of air.

"This is my bedroom," I said. "Sorry. I didn't mean to bring you with me. I'm still getting the hang of this whole thing."

He started to shake his head, and he gripped my shoulder tighter. It was a bit painful, to be honest. Malik was strong.

"What the *fuck*, Cole?" His voice got louder with every word. He was practically yelling.

"Shh," I said, raising both my hands, palms out, in what I hoped was a good "calm down" gesture. I waited, but I didn't hear any noise. After a couple of seconds of nothing, I exhaled. I'd beaten my folks home. "Okay, they're not home yet. That's good." I winced. "Malik, you're kind of breaking my shoulder."

He finally let go. He also blinked, and it seemed to set off a whole series of blinking, like he was making up for all the blinks he'd missed. He looked wobbly.

"Maybe sit down," I said, but he was already tipping. I managed to half catch him, and we landed on my bed.

"I feel awful," he said.

"I was like that my first couple of times, too," I said. My heart was hammering in my chest. This was so bad. I mean, escaping those creepy suit people was one thing—and hey, let's just unpack *that* for a moment, because there were creepy suit people after me—but I'd just teleported Malik from his bedroom to mine. If that wasn't awkward enough, he looked like he was going to pass out. Unconscious Malik in my bed?

I *so* did not have a plan for this.

Malik shook his head again, harder. "What just happened?"

I took a breath. "I know it sounds crazy, but I was trying to teleport back here and you grabbed me. You, uh—well, I think you kind of hitched a ride."

He looked around my room like he was trying to make himself believe it. "Teleport."

"It started happening two weeks ago," I said.

He tilted his head back. He stared at my ceiling like it would provide some sort of answer to what was happening. It apparently didn't.

"You teleport," he said.

At least this time it didn't sound like he thought I was certifiable. That was progress, right?

"I teleport. That's how I got in your window. I swear I wasn't trying to get in your window, it's just sometimes I go off target. It's annoying, actually, and—"

He held up one hand. I stopped talking.

"You *teleport*."

I nodded. "Yes." The broken record thing was understandable, but it was getting annoying, cute boy or not. I had bigger problems. Creepy suit brain-melty problems. Him repeating the obvious wasn't helpful. *Please don't freak out*, I thought.

The thing happened again. Like a breath of air passing between us, cold against the back of my neck and making all the hairs on my arm stand up.

What *was* that?

Malik shook his head and looked at me again. He seemed calmer. That was good. "I'm trying to be cool here. It's..." He didn't seem to have a word for it.

"Yeah," I said.

He laughed. It started low, but it got loud, fast. He had a great laugh, which I already knew, but this was the first time I'd been right beside him while he did it. Some of the terror of the last little while seemed to drain out of my chest, and I started to laugh with him. Creepy suit guys chasing me down, leaping through windows… In the face of the laughter of Malik King, it wasn't so bad.

Except it really should be bad. Maybe I was just hysterical? Whatever. Laughing felt good.

He looked around again and seemed to take stock. "This is your room, huh?"

"Yeah."

"You're really tidy."

"Hey, your room was tidy." I thought about it. "Is tidy bad?"

He shook his head. Then he yawned. "Sorry," he said. "I'm wrecked."

"Yeah. It's like that at first. That's why I passed out in the hallway at school."

He looked at me, surprised. "You mean after…your locker?"

"Yeah, I teleported into my locker."

He frowned. "Why?"

"I didn't do it on *purpose*. I was trying to get back to the school from the museum."

"The museum?"

"That was the first…" I shook my head. "You know what? It doesn't matter. Yes, I teleported into my locker. But it was an accident."

I heard a sound downstairs. The front door. Holy crap, I'd cut that close. I held up one hand, and Malik nodded. I went to my door, cracking it open.

"That you, Mom?" I called.

"Yes, we're home. Did you forget to turn the light on for us?"

"Sorry!" I said. I mean, I hadn't forgotten, exactly, what with all the abduction. "Did you guys have a good night?"

"Yes." They were coming up the stairs. I waved wildly behind me and then, realizing I didn't look like a kid who'd been asleep a few seconds ago, I stripped off my shirt, kicked off my shoes, and shucked my jeans and socks. I probably broke a record, but I was standing in my boxers by the time my folks were visible from my doorway.

"Gonna go back to bed," I said and signed to my father.

Good night, he signed back.

"Good night, sweetheart," my mother said.

They both looked really happy. Definitely a good Date Night. My father put his hand on my mother's back as they passed my door. I closed it and exhaled, resting my head against the wood for a second.

When I turned around, I didn't see Malik anywhere.

"Malik?" I whispered.

His head popped up from the far side of my bed. I couldn't help it, I snickered.

He scowled at me, then stood up. His boxers had sort of ridden down, and I forced my gaze back up to his face. No part of Malik was not hot. He blinked a couple of times, then sat down on my bed, quickly.

"Are you okay?" I asked.

He looked at me. "How do I get home?"

I looked anxiously back at my door. My parents would take a little while to get ready for bed. "Um, I can try to teleport us back in a bit."

"Right. Teleport." He shook his head, then lay back across my bed, looking up at the ceiling. After a second of standing there feeling really dumb and *really* exposed in my boxers, I did the same. Our feet hung off the edge. I waited for him to say something. I wondered if maybe I should explain from the beginning. At least that would pass some time while we waited for my folks to be well and truly asleep. But when I turned to him to start, his eyes were closed and he was fast asleep.

I nudged his shoulder. Nothing.

Seriously the cutest boy in the school. It was almost enough to make me rethink caring about sports.

I nudged him again, and again nothing. He was out cold. I remembered how I'd crashed after my first trips to and from the museum, and faced facts.

The cute boy in my bed wasn't going to wake up short of dynamite.

Instead, I managed to pull him up onto the bed and flipped my half of the blanket over him. He didn't wake up for that, so I officially gave up and lay down beside him. It was warm enough that I'd be fine if I got under the sheet. I turned off the light and wished I could pass out just as easily.

The whole insane night replayed in my head. It made for a pretty awful list of plusses and minuses.

There were other people like me. Teleporters. On the surface, that was a plus.

But the other teleporters didn't seem like nice people, and they were after me. And had "institutions." That was a minus.

They knew enough about where I was to ambush me in my own

house—big minus—and seemed to be able to sort of pull me with them whether or not I wanted to go—giant minus. Also? They could melt brains, and they wore suits. When had guys in suits ever turned out to be a good thing? Never. Never is when. Biggest minus ever.

I had no idea what to do. Yet another minus.

Malik King was sleeping in my bed, right beside me, and I had no idea what we'd do in the morning, what with how my parents lived here and stuff. Huge, red-alert level minus.

I looked at him again. Even in the dark I could see the outline of his face. Good jawline.

Okay, so maybe there was a little bit of a plus to this.

I groaned and tried to force my brain to slow down so I could sleep. Just before I finally drifted off, I thought of one more thing: I might not have any idea what to do, but I was pretty sure Malik believed me. Seeing was believing. Or, well, teleporting was.

I wasn't on my own.

That might be the biggest plus yet.

TWENTY-TWO

U h, Cole?"
        The thing about having a slow and gentle alarm clock was you got used to ignoring it. It helped that it also played the sound of a beach and slowly added seagulls, too, but it had a snooze button, which I think I'd already hammered twice on reflex until…

"Cole?"

I went from groggy and sleepy to wide awake in about half a second. I opened my eyes, and sure enough, I wasn't alone in my room. Malik King was awake and still in my bed, though he'd kicked most of the blanket off. My clock was doing the seagull thing again. What time was it?

"Shit," I said.

"Yeah." Malik rubbed his face. "Shit." He looked at me. "So…" He swallowed. "I'm…We…You…"

I exhaled. "We need to get you home."

His eyebrow rose. "This happened. This…" He waved one hand. He'd sat up on his elbow, which did really nice things to his arm, and I tried not to stare. "You can teleport."

Oh, great. Back to that. "Yep."

He shook his head. "See, when you just say it like that, it sounds…"

I nodded. "I know. Trust me."

Malik swallowed. "Okay. So…" He glanced at my clock. "I've got maybe half an hour before I need to get ready for work."

"Okay." I sat up and swung my legs around and realized my number one priority was now keeping my back to Malik because it was morning, and I was a guy and…Well. Yeah. Current plan? Keeping my back to Malik until I could, y'know, *calm down*. I went to my closet, grabbed some jeans, and made myself far less comfortable but also way less likely to die of complete embarrassment. I wondered if he was having the same problem.

Okay, thinking about *that* was not going to help.

I tugged on a T-shirt, grabbed socks, and tracked down my shoes from where I'd kicked them aside last night. "Okay. Next stop, your room."

Malik was just staring at me. He'd gotten out of my bed and was standing there, looking both super hot in just a pair of boxers but also really uncomfortable because, probably, just a pair of boxers.

"How…?" he asked.

"I think you just need to be touching me."

His eyebrow rose. He even smiled, just a little bit.

I felt my face burning.

"Touching you."

Was he teasing me? It felt like he was teasing me.

"That's how it worked last time," I said. My voice sort of wobbled.

Malik nodded. The awkwardness rose a few hundred levels. It *really* didn't help that he was in his boxers.

"Okay," I said. "Ready for a ride?" The moment the words were out, I wanted to take them back, but Malik grinned, shrugging.

"I just grab on to you?" he said.

I nodded. "I use the door," I said. "So hold on to me and wait for me to move, and walk with me, and you'll come with me." I tried to sound confident, even though I was anything but. I mean, I'd brought someone with me on a teleport exactly once. By accident. Last night.

We stood in front of my door, Malik a half step behind me. He reached out and put his hand on my shoulder, and it made me warm all over. He held on a bit tighter than maybe he needed to, but then again, he'd had a death grip on me last night, too, so maybe that mattered.

Also, was his hand shaking? Or was that me?

I opened my door as slowly as I could. Silence from my parents' room. Thank the gods for Date Night. Saturdays we generally slept in. I fended for myself for breakfast, usually.

I closed my eyes and tried to remember everything I could from my brief visit to Malik's room, but I couldn't remember a whole lot more than the carpet and the sight of Malik staring at me and the sound of his father's voice.

I could feel the tug. The doorway was definitely ready to send me somewhere. I had a brief moment of panic that I'd end up somewhere with the creepy-ass guys in suits, then resolutely forced that idea from my mind. No. Malik's room. Malik's room. Malik's room. No trips *anywhere* else. Of course, the moment I thought about anywhere else, the sheer volume of every other possible place I could end up started to crowd into my head. It was like trying not to think about a pink elephant.

We stepped forward together, and I tried to force the rest of the world out of my head except for Malik's room.

Poof.

And something else.

❖

I had maybe half a second to feel some triumph over hitting my target before I collapsed onto Malik's bedroom floor, landing hard on my knees. Malik fell with me, knocking me sprawling. I barely felt his weight on top of me. I was too distracted by the light strobing behind my eyelids.

Everywhere and everything seemed to be colliding in my head.

"Cole?" His voice sounded far away, like it was echoing down a giant series of hallways, each hallway connected to another dozen hallways.

I was everywhere, all at once. I was at school and I was at home and I was at the museum and I was in my locker and I was—

"Cole!" Malik's face swam into view. His dark brown eyes caught me first, then the rest of him came back into focus. The pulses of twisting, pulling and yanking fell away. I was with Malik. In his bedroom. He'd gotten off me and was crouching in front of me. When had I sat up?

"There," I said. "See?" I blinked the last few flashes of light from my eyes. "No problem."

"Malik?" The voice came from the other side of Malik's bedroom door. It was a woman. His mother?

Malik pointed, and it took me a second to realize he was giving me a direction. I struggled to my feet, rubbery, and looked where he was pointing.

I exhaled. "Really?"

His glare said this wasn't open to argument, so I yanked open the door and hid in Malik's closet.

I barely got in before he reached past me, snatched a pair of jeans, and then closed the door on my back. I heard his bedroom door open, and I froze, barely even breathing.

"You're going to be late." A very familiar tone of reproach mixed with love. Mom voice. Definitely his mother.

"Sorry. I overslept."

"Do you need a ride?"

"Oh, my God, yes please. You're the best."

"I know this." A pause. "Are you all right?"

"I didn't sleep well."

"Well, don't forget to eat. You've got ten minutes. You, me, and the car."

"Thanks."

I waited, unsure if I should come back out of the closet—*sigh*—or not. Malik opened the doors, and I turned around.

"That was incredible. Are you okay? You seemed sort of out of it."

"I…" Whatever had happened, it had scared the crap out of me, but I felt more or less okay now. How many times had I had the crap scared out of me lately? I should be out of crap. Or whatever. "Yeah. Not used to bringing passengers."

He reached past me for a shirt. "I can't believe I have to go to work. How can I go to work? I just freaking teleported."

He pulled his work shirt over his head and then stopped, staring at me. Malik worked at the grocery store. How did I not know that?

"What?" he said.

"I don't know," I said, but it mustn't have sounded convincing.

"Dude," he said. "What?"

"It's just…You're kind of taking this well."

He shrugged. "It was cool. I'm not gonna freak out. And I don't want to be late for work."

"Wasn't so cool when I got stuck in my locker."

He did the one eyebrow thing again. "You seem to be getting the hang of it, though, right?"

"It's been a rough couple of weeks."

His mother called from downstairs. His name, drawn out into roughly three extra syllables.

Malik winced. "I gotta go. Are you…" He waved his hand at his room. "Are you gonna be okay? Like…to get home?"

I nodded. "Once you go, I'll use your door. To get to my door."

He grinned. "See? That? That's cool."

I wondered if he also remembered I'd been snatched by creepy freaks. But still, he had a contagious smile, and he flashed it at me one more time before he closed his closet door on my face again.

I stood in the dark for a few seconds. I heard him leave his room, and then I counted to thirty. I snuck out of the closet—*sigh*, again—and went to his door. All bravado and "it's cool!" aside, I wasn't too keen on a repeat performance of whatever the hell had happened on the way here.

Which had been *what*, exactly? *Everywhere*. It had been *everywhere*. I'd been trying so hard to think about Malik's bedroom that I'd been thinking about everywhere else, too.

I took a deep breath and reached for the door handle. I pictured my own bedroom in my head, and the sense connection was there almost immediately. In fact, it was crazy strong and really eager to get going. I could feel the tug, but more than that, it was specific. Like, it *felt* like my room.

And beyond that…There was something beyond that…

I closed my eyes, and for just a second, that overwhelming feeling of too-much-too-fast-flashing-lights returned. I pulled back, and it stopped. The more I did this, the worse it got.

Or maybe…maybe it was getting *better*?

"Just go home," I said. Finding that sense of my own bedroom was just as easy as it had been a few seconds ago, and I opened the door and went home.

Poof.

❖

My mother was yawning in the hallway, still in her robe, and she smiled when she saw me step out of my room. I'd intended to land on the other side of the door, inside my bedroom, but other than that, it had felt just about effortless.

"Hey, kiddo," she said. "You're up and about early. Big plans for the day?"

I thought about that. Last night I'd been kidnapped, had something done to my brain, barely gotten out with said brain intact, had an accidental sleepover with Malik-freaking-King, and I had final exams starting Monday. My bullet journal had way, way more unfilled squares than ever before, and I hadn't even added any since yesterday, what with all the kidnapping and stuff. At the very least, I'd need to stop and come up with some sort of plan because my life was completely out of control.

"I've got a lot on my plate," I said.

My mother smiled. "Well, you know what you can handle. But if you need help, you just ask us."

I nodded. "Okay."

She turned, heading for the stairs. She was probably going to go turn on the coffee. She and my dad did the coffee-in-bed thing on Saturdays.

"Hey, Mom?" I said.

She paused, turning to look up at me.

"If you could go anywhere..." I said. "Where would you go?"

"Can I take you and your dad with me?"

Good question. I knew I could handle one person. Could I handle two? "Sure. I mean, I think so. Let's say yes."

"Well. In that case? I'd take you both to England." She'd been born there, but she'd moved to Canada when she was ten. She tilted her head. Uh-oh. Mom radar detected. "Why do you ask?"

"It's just something that's been on my mind."

She looked at me for a moment, and I resisted the urge to squirm. "Cole, you *do* know that you don't have to be an interpreter, right?"

What? I blinked. This again? Where was this coming from? "But I like it." And I was good at it. And it was important. And it had been my plan for...like...ever.

She came back up the stairs and leaned against the wall. "I know that. Your father does, too. I just want to be clear about it, though. If you wanted to study something else, you know we'd be okay with that, right?" She met my gaze. "Both of us would be. You can take time to decide things, like your friend Malik."

"I know," I said. Except I didn't. I *hated* the thought. Like, why were they both so down on me doing what Dad does? I didn't get it. "Do you think I'm doing the wrong thing?" I asked. "Linguistics, I mean?"

She shook her head. "Not even a little. I just don't want you to focus too much on one thing. You're good at that." She said it with a little smile, though, so it didn't feel entirely like a jab. "I don't doubt you can do almost anything someone can learn. I just want you to consider your options. We'd be okay with anything else you'd like to do."

My chest felt tight, and my throat had this little pain in the back, like I couldn't swallow right. This was way, way too close to a "we're proud of you" moment, and those always made me feel like bawling. It was time to eject.

"Well, the good news is I want to be an interpreter," I said. "So no one has to be okay with anything else."

She nodded and smiled, but she had one of those mom-looks that told me we were totally going to end up talking about this again, and likely sooner rather than later.

"Do you want me to go turn on the coffeemaker?" I said. "I can set it up before I go."

She nodded. "That would be wonderful. You heading out?" I could tell she wanted to ask me for every detail about that, but she held herself back. My parents were getting way better at that.

"I have some things I need to get and some stuff I need to do." I tried not to flinch. Could I possibly be more vague? Maybe if I put on an "ask me no questions" T-shirt or threw a smoke bomb at my feet.

But all Mom said was, "Okay. You okay on your own?" I could practically hear her forcing herself not to push or ask more questions.

"I'm good."

"Do you need a ride?"

"Actually," I said, looking my mother right in the eyes and fighting off a hysterical laugh, "I really don't."

❖

I paused to brush my teeth and do something with my hair that didn't say "crash-landed through a window" and then went downstairs. I almost forgot to set the coffee machine going, which would have ended badly for my child-of-the-year chances, and I tossed a banana and some granola bars into my bag. My phone, which had spent the night beside the front door, was only a third charged, so I shoved the charger into my bag along with everything else.

The smell of coffee was starting to spread through the house. I nodded to myself. If I was going to try this, I needed to get started. Pretty soon at least one of my parents would come downstairs.

I regarded my front door. I'd been on the outside of the house with my back to the open door when I'd been grabbed. How had they known where I'd be? Had they been following me? I tried to remember if anyone else had been on the street last night, but I had no idea. I wasn't paying attention at the time.

Ignoring this didn't work. I'd thought maybe they were tracking me somehow when I teleported, but now I knew they could teleport too. New plan.

Uh.

Any second now, I'd come up with a new plan.

My stomach rumbled. Okay, so maybe I should have some breakfast first.

Wait.

I looked back into the kitchen and saw the unused pizza money from last night on the counter. I got it, then came back to the front door.

Okay. New plan? If they could pop in whenever they wanted, I needed to figure out how to be just as good.

Remembering the craziness of this morning's teleport back to Malik's house, I hesitated, reaching out for the door until just my fingertips brushed the door handle. As soon as they touched, it was there. The tugs, waiting to take me somewhere, but also, beyond that I felt…*something.*

I frowned and touched the handle a bit more. The more my skin touched the cool metal, the stronger the feeling.

The tug began as normal, like I was standing shoulder-deep in water, but it only pulled me from the center of my chest. Instead of it being a single pull, it was more like the pull was going every which way at once. When I took a moment to consider that, it shifted, and one tug grew stronger than all the others. It was all very faint, and it didn't even make me think I should lean to counterbalance, but it was there.

I had an instinct I was getting better at this, but I wasn't sure at all what *this* was.

I bit my lip and stopped when I felt the scab from where I'd fallen. The locker and the museum seemed like forever ago, rather than two weeks ago Monday.

At the thought, the tug shifted twice, and this time the tugs were strong enough I did lean back. Each lurch had felt *familiar*, too.

I let go of the door and took a step back.

The museum. The locker.

That's what I'd felt. The door starting to *connect* me to them. I'd barely had to think about it at all. Something had seriously changed. I wondered if it had anything to do with my jaunt with Malik or nearly getting brain-fried by Beardy McBeardface.

I put my hand back on the door handle and tried again.

The museum.

Lurch to the left, and then a constant pull. I could just let go and be on my way.

My locker.

A dropping sensation. I carefully let go of the door handle again.

My stomach growled again, louder. I grinned, grabbed the door handle, and remembered a trip into Ottawa I'd had with my dad last summer. We'd gone to this all-night diner on Elgin Street for breakfast, and it had great waffles. They'd swum in syrup.

I'd been kidnapped and had to jump out a window to escape.

Cole Tozer, Badass deserved waffles.

I opened the door, took a step, and was gone.

❖

With a giant stack of waffles in syrup, even the biggest of life's problems could be put into perspective. I had my bullet journal open, and I'd carried more than a few things forward onto this newest list, but that was okay. I was pretty much out of study time, but my applications were already out there, and my grades were good. Even if I somehow bombed my exams—like, *nuclear* level bombed—I'd be okay. I'd done the math, and there was no way I was walking out of my exams with a zero, so...

I paused, realizing I had teleported to a diner more than an hour away from my house, and I was eating waffles and telling myself it was okay not to ace my exams because I had bigger stuff to worry about, namely the teleporting freaks in suits who wanted to melt my brain.

Last Week Cole would not recognize Today Cole. And I was pretty sure Today Cole might be losing his mind a little bit.

On my list, I'd just written "Freaks." It was a little word with a big meaning, and other than the little square box beside it—all ready to be colored in once I dealt with it, which was optimistic to say the least—it didn't look like much. Study for calculus, ask Alec about his date, find out if Candice is willing to host a Rainbow Club party, and deal with kidnappers. No problem. Check, check, check. Calm and collected? My middle names.

The door opened, and I jerked my head up to look, nearly knocking my milk over.

Okay, maybe I wasn't so calm after all. I shivered even though I wasn't cold, but a woman in a long black skirt with a short crop of dyed blue hair came in, not Beardy or Freckle-Face or Mr. Stiff. I went back to my waffles and tried to shake off the bone-deep shudder.

Maybe it was just because a door was opening nearby, but I'd had that tug-and-snap feeling. I'd been almost sure I'd look over and see the three men standing there, ready for Brain Melt Part Two: Brain Meltier.

Then the blue-haired woman slid into the booth right across from me.

Oh, crap.

I stared. She stared right back. She was kind of intimidating. She was looking down at me, I was pretty sure, which meant she was taller than me. Granted, that wasn't hard, but I got the impression she could look down at people no matter how tall they were. She wasn't a fan of the sun, if the paleness of her skin was any indication. She had two eyebrow rings and a little silver stud in her nose. She was pretty, but more than a bit scary. Her eye makeup gave her this *sharp* look. Older than me, definitely, but I wasn't sure by how much. She could have been in her twenties, maybe? The blue hair was the most obvious thing, but she also had tattoos all over her right arm. Doors, keys, and keyholes spun up her arm and vanished into the sleeve of her T-shirt. Her T-shirt was blue, with a silhouette of a witch on a broom with a cat and the words "Witch Delivery Service." She'd cut the neckline out and made it into a V-neck.

"Can I get you something?" The waiter had arrived, and I hadn't even noticed.

Her smile transformed her whole face. "Coffee?" she said. She had an accent I didn't recognize.

The waiter left.

"You're buying me coffee," she said.

"Okay," I said. Between the tattoos of the doors and the accent, I was pretty sure I was face-to-face with another freak. "Uh. Who are you?"

She stared at me some more. It made me want to wipe my face.

"How old are you, anyway?" she asked. "Fourteen?"

Okay, older or not, freak or not, that shit was *not* okay. "I'm seventeen." I tilted my head. "Why? You're what? Forty?"

She grinned. "Sorry."

I stabbed a piece of waffle. I was full, but it was still a waffle.

The waiter came back with her coffee and she poured way, way too much sugar into it. I watched as whole seconds went by with the stuff pouring from the canister.

"Okay," she said. "Here's the thing. You're new and you're good. But you're also *loud*. You're gonna attract some unwanted attention, I'll bet, and you need to know about it."

I glanced back at the door. I hadn't been crazy. I'd *felt* her arrive.

She gave me a little nod and sipped her coffee.

"You're not with those guys in suits?" I said.

She put her coffee down. "You've already seen them?"

"They snatched me from my house," I said, and then we both cringed because I said it way too loud. We looked around, but none of the other early-morning visitors seemed to care I was discussing my abduction. No one cared I'd been kidnapped.

See? I couldn't wait to move to Ottawa. A freak could be anonymous here.

She leaned forward. "And you got away?" A little line formed between her eyebrows. My mother got that line. That line meant she didn't believe me.

"They tried to melt my brain, but it didn't work. I used a window before round two."

"You jumped out a window?" Her eyes were wide, and she looked impressed.

It bothered me how good that made me feel.

"Not out, so much as…y'know…*through*." I waved a hand. "I used the window instead of a door. To…*travel*. Got back to my bedroom." Eventually. She didn't need to know about the misfire or my unintended passenger.

Her mouth was open, and she was staring at me.

Now I felt less good.

"What's wrong?" I said.

"You're *seventeen*?" she said.

"Y'know," I said, "you guys all seem really fixated on the whole age thing. Beardy McBeardface was all 'I'm gonna lock your brain until you're older, kid.' I have a driver's license. I'm allowed to drive massive chunks of metal on roads at high speeds. I'm even going to be allowed to vote soon, so maybe I'm old enough to…" I dropped my voice, which had been rising again. "Teleport."

She took another swig of her coffee syrup. She was fighting off another grin, but I could tell it was close because she got dimples.

"Lexa," she said, putting the cup down.

I blinked. "What?"

"My name," she said. "It's Lexa."

Lexa with the blue hair held out her hand. I shook it.

"I'm Cole," I said.

"Nice to meet you, Cole. I need to go open my gallery, but I'll find you again." She glanced around. "Is this a place you come to often?"

I shook my head. "No. I just wanted to practice, and I was hungry." That little line was back between her eyebrows.

"If you ask me how old I am again, I'm totally not going to pay for your coffee," I said.

"I bet you're giving them fits," she said. "Okay. Quick and dirty tips. Don't hang out near a door you've used to travel. You are *so* loud. It's easy to feel you. That'll throw them off at least. And when you do *use* a door, use another one right away. Like skipping a stone. Four or five times and even their best will have a hard time figuring out where you ended up. Especially if the doors are near each other. It gets confusing."

"Who are they?"

"Bureaucrats," she said, with a sour smile. "People who think muses like us should follow their rules. They think they know what's best, so our input isn't always welcome."

"Muses?" I said.

She downed the last of her coffee. "We inspire people, and we can show up anywhere." She winked. "What would you call it?"

"I've been going with 'freak,'" I said. *Inspire people?*

Lexa laughed. "All the best muses are freaks." She got up. "I'll find you again," she said. "Maybe later this afternoon." She checked her watch. "In, say, six hours."

That was a weird way to put it. I looked at my phone and did the math. "Okay."

"We can meet back here," she said. "Just try to keep it down in the meanwhile."

"I don't know how to do that." Panic rose in my chest. "They grabbed me from my own house."

She scowled. "I'll see what I can do. Just stay clear of doorways. You're loud, like I said. But if you're near a door that you've used, try to picture it in here." She tapped her temple. "And *lock* it."

I shook my head. I had no idea what she was talking about.

"Just try it," she said. "I really do need to go. I have an artist... Anyway. I'm sorry. Just keep dodging them. I'll find you later." And she was off. I watched her go and kept my eyes on her as she opened the door to the diner. I wanted to see it. It wasn't really anything, though

I felt a distant tug-and-snap, almost like an echo in my chest. Lexa walked through the door like anyone would. But she never showed up on the other side of the glass. No one in the diner so much as raised an eyebrow. No one on the street passing by so much as missed a step.

She was just gone.

Just keep dodging them. As advice went, it was not exactly Charles Xavier–level stuff. Where was James McAvoy when you needed him?

"Anything else?" The waiter was back.

"No, I'm good. Thanks," I said.

"She's pretty," the waiter said, nodding at the door.

"She's a muse," I said.

He laughed like I said something funny, then left to go get me my bill.

TWENTY-THREE

From the diner on Elgin Street in Ottawa, I teleported to the corner store. It occurred to me at the last second I'd need to consider if places were open or not. Otherwise I could end up on the wrong side of a locked and alarmed door. From there, I poofed my way to the public bathrooms down by the locks.

Every teleport brought back that feeling of a corridor full of corridors, and I was starting to get it. They were options. I could feel all the different places I could go, and for the first time it was really sinking in that I could go *anywhere*.

It was kind of awesome. It was also overwhelming, so I decided to play it safe and cut it short.

Pausing just a second in the bathrooms to catch my breath, I turned right back around again and aimed for home.

And misfired.

Wrong home. *Again.* I stood in the yard of the house we used to live in when I was a kid. What it was about this place that seemed to override my attempts to go home to my own house? Was it just history? This was my first home, so this was somehow *more* home? That didn't seem right. At least this time I'd ended up on the outside rather than the inside.

I glanced around, but no one was watching. I bit my lip and tried the front door.

It was locked.

Which meant I couldn't use it to get anywhere else. I considered my options and decided the closest door would likely be down by the locks, back at the public restroom I'd used to poof here. It would be faster than walking all the way home.

I was just about to start walking when I felt it. It started as a shiver, and I turned and glanced back at the front door of the house I used to live in as the shiver grew. It was the tug, and there would be a snap.

I put my hand against the door. My sense of the everywhere of doors and connections popped up right away, and I also had this feeling of something coming fast right at me. It was like a firework spinning its way toward me, about to deliver a loud bang right to my face. Remembering what Lexa had said at the diner, I imagined the door locked up tight and sort of *pushed* at the door with my head, as though I could slam it shut with will alone.

It worked just in time. I rocked back with a mental thud, my brain registering the inbound teleporter *bouncing* off the door. No other way to describe it. Whoever had been about to end up right beside me ricocheted somewhere else instead. I didn't see any outward sign of it. No dramatic shaking of the door or anything. It was all just a change of pressure in my head.

My ears even popped.

I was pretty sure I was right. I kind of swayed and had to take a second to breathe. Locking doors was a bit of a whammy to the noggin, apparently. Still, I couldn't help but smile. I wondered what it felt like to try to go somewhere and get deflected. On the off chance it was Freckle-Face or Beardy, I hoped it was at least a little painful.

I waited a few moments longer, but nothing happened, so I reached out and touched the door again.

Nothing. In fact, I couldn't feel even the slightest draw from the door. I *pushed*, and there was some give, and the sense that everywhere might be behind the block if I pushed hard enough but...nope. Besides, I didn't want to undo whatever I just did.

Locking the door for them locked me out, too. Huh. I wondered how long it would take to wear off. It was just a gut feeling, but I was pretty sure this wasn't a permanent thing.

Either way, given that I'd attracted attention, maybe it was time to go home and call it a morning for teleportation practice before someone saw me skulking in front of my old house. I had six hours until I could meet up with Lexa again. Maybe I should go over my biology notes.

"My life is weird," I said.

I started walking.

❖

Again.

I replayed the conversation.

"We need to relock your gift again."

Beardy had said *again*. And then he'd twitched like he'd made a mistake.

I crossed the street and shoved my hands in my pockets. They'd said they were going to bury my memories. That false memory of burning alive in the museum, that would definitely have been traumatic, and Beardy seemed to think my brain would just repress it. And with it, my so-called "gift" and my memory of teleporting to the museum. I wondered what kind of fallout would have happened had he given me traumatic memories of my locker and Malik's room and every other accidental trip across town I'd taken. I'd have holes in my memory, but would I still have the rest of it? Or would everything from the last two weeks to now just be *gone*? I'd already lived through that kind of thing once, and I—

"Oh my God."

I stopped walking.

Mrs. Easton. Colenap.

"We need to relock your gift again."

Again.

My heart was hammering in my chest. But…it made sense. I'd been a kid, and I'd been found at Mrs. Easton's house. Everyone had assumed she'd kidnapped me, even when she swore she hadn't. She'd sworn she hadn't even known I'd been in her backyard. She'd sworn the door was locked.

How else could I have gotten there? I was too small to climb a fence. I couldn't have gotten that far from the last time I'd been seen without someone grabbing me in a car. My feet were clean.

Except.

Except I *could*. Cole Tozer very much could get across town in a blink of an eye.

I'd been found asleep in her backyard beside a locked door, and she'd all but broken down trying to get people to believe that she hadn't snatched me. The only reason she didn't get jail time was that I was unharmed.

That and the fact I couldn't remember anything other than waking up with some cats.

Did Beardy—or whoever was the Beardy back then—pop in to give me a mind-wipe?

There was no way to know, but it felt right.

Like, for the first time ever I felt like maybe I had it right about what had happened to me. It was more than just an instinct.

It also pissed me off.

I started walking again, angry enough I was almost stomping my way down the sidewalk. I'd been branded an outcast for years because of that one afternoon, and if the teleporting freaks thought I was up for a second round, they were way off.

There would be no melting of Cole Tozer's brain. Not now. Not ever.

By the time I made it to the park, I'd stopped swearing under my breath and I wasn't clenching my fists anymore. I got to the public bathroom door and grabbed it with purpose.

The maze of everywhere beyond my fingertips snapped to attention, like it had been waiting all along for me to get mad. It burned into my head, and I knew I wasn't just being loud. I was *deafening*. The longer I held the door, the angrier I got. At even the briefest thought of a place, the memory of it flew through the connections and told me: Here. This one. This was the museum. This was Malik's bedroom. This is your room. This is your old house.

This is Mrs. Easton's backyard.

They did this to me once already. They wanted to do it again.

To hell with them.

Home, I told the door. *Not my old one. The real one. Now.*

Poof.

❖

I was five hours into the six-hour countdown to seeing Lexa-with-the-blue-hair again, and I was still pretty pissed. I'd dragged my biology notes out and taken over half the couch. My mom was sitting in her chair reading. She asked me to either stop sighing or to go to my room, so I let it go and tried not to stare at my phone, waiting for the last hour to go by without being impatient. It wasn't working, but at least my mother wasn't annoyed at me making noise anymore.

My phone pinged.

It was Malik. *I'm done work. You free?*

I glanced up. My mom had been rereading one of her Dita Wallace books for the last few hours. My dad was doing something on his computer in his office.

"If I wanted to go hang out with a friend for a while, would that be okay?" I said. "I'll be home for dinner."

"Malik?" My mother lowered her book, and the smile she aimed at me was so over-the-top I wanted to crawl into the sofa cushions.

"Yes," I said, my face burning. "Malik."

"Sure," my mother said with another big smile. "Keep in touch. And have fun."

Gah. Parents.

Yep, I sent. *Where are you?*

Still at work. Just finished.

I got up and grabbed my jacket. I eyed my front door warily, considering, and then remembered how angry I was at the teleporting brain-melters, and with a deeply felt *to hell with them*, I poofed my way to the grocery store. Effortless. Some switch had definitely been flipped. Outside the grocery store, Malik had his back to me, still looking at his phone.

"Hey," I said.

Malik turned around, doing a double take. "Did you just...?"

I nodded. "I'm sort of practicing."

He stared at me.

I stared back.

"Uh, so," I said, thinking maybe poofing in was sort of overeager and a little bit sad. "How was work?"

He laughed. "Really? You do your...*thing*...and you want to know how work was?"

"Hey, there's no cool moment I can't make awkward," I said.

He laughed. "You know what? You—"

I didn't get to find out what. Because with a triple burst of staccato pops I could feel behind my rib cage, we weren't alone.

I whirled on my heel. All three of the brain melters were standing outside the grocery store.

I hadn't locked the damn door. I was such an idiot.

TWENTY-FOUR

"W e need to go," I said, grabbing Malik's arm.

"Cole?" he said. He eyed the three men.

Beardy McBeardface scowled at me, then looked at Malik with way too much attention.

"Keep the hell away from me," I said.

Freckle-Face took a step forward, but Beardy put his hand out, stopping him.

I gave Malik's arm a little tug. "Come on," I said. I pulled him away, and he walked with me. I kept my head turned, watching the three men.

They didn't follow us, though they did take a couple of steps forward to keep us in their line of sight for the first little while. That wasn't creepy in the slightest, oh no. Finally, they dropped out of view, which was great. I pointed ahead.

"Let's go around the corner," I said, "and then we can—"

But that plan needed to be scrapped right off. Once we'd hooked around the corner, we didn't go three steps before I saw Beardy McBeardface coming out of the pharmacy, two doors down.

"Cole?" Malik said again. He sounded freaked. I didn't blame him.

"These are the guys who grabbed me," I said. I looked around. Where were the other two?

Beardy got to the sidewalk and then stopped. He was definitely in the way.

"What do we do?" Malik said.

Good question. I was fingerspelling like mad. *Door. Door. Door.* We were right in the middle of a whole bunch of businesses. There wasn't a block in any direction that didn't have enough doorways for

Beardy and the brain-melters to use. No matter which way I tried to go with Malik, they'd be able to skip ahead of us.

Wait.

What had Lexa said?

Like skipping a rock.

"Do you trust me?" I said. I glanced at the pharmacy door meaningfully.

Malik looked at me. Nodded.

I held out my hand, and he took it, squeezing a bit tighter than maybe necessary.

Beardy didn't take long to clue in. He opened his mouth as though he wanted to yell something at me, then closed it, starting for us. Malik and I all but ran. Beardy tried to get between us, but Malik gave him a rough shove and we were past him. We hit the pharmacy door.

Poof.

Malik tried to let go of my hand outside the public bathrooms by the locks, but I shook my head. I could already feel them. Just being close to the door, I had this *sense* of them. Pressure in my skull. I could lock it, maybe.

No, no time.

"We need to keep going. They can follow," I said, then pushed on the door again, pulling Malik with me.

Poof.

Candice smiled at us, noticed we were holding hands, and then offered me a big grin for about half a second before the smile slipped off her face.

"You okay, Cole?"

I probably looked like a lunatic.

"Just need to use your bathroom," I said, dragging Malik through Meeples.

"Thanks!" Malik called out behind us.

We hit the bathroom door.

Poof.

The music room at school.

Poof.

The Inn.

Poof.

Poof.

Poof.

Poof.

"Cole!"

Malik's voice made me stop. We were outside the town library. I'd lost track of how many doors we'd used.

Malik shook his head, and I finally let go of his hand. He took a step back, leaning against the wall of the library and taking deep breaths. He looked like he was going to hurl.

"One sec," I said, turning to the library doors. Looking through the glass, it didn't look like anyone was about to come through, so I pressed my hands against them.

The whole of everywhere was beneath my fingertips. And so was the feeling of other people doing exactly what I was doing—touching everywhere, and looking, feeling for something, or someone.

For me.

I pushed with my mind, hard. Slamming and locking the library doors.

Everywhere vanished.

"Okay," I said. Malik looked a bit better.

"That was incredible," he said. He blinked a few times.

"Are you okay?"

"Honestly? I kinda want to barf."

"Sorry," I said.

My phone pinged. I blinked and pulled it out.

It was a text from my dad. *Almost dinner time*, it said. I looked at the clock. "Holy crap."

I was panting. Malik raised his eyebrow.

"Sorry, I'm just..." I shook my head. "I'm not sure..." I waved a hand around.

I felt another "pop" again and turned in time to see Freckle-Face step out from beside the library. Right. Staff entrance. Damnit.

"You need to come with us," Freckle-Face said. He sounded pissed. "*Both* of you."

Oh, hell no.

I grabbed Malik's hand, and we bolted again. He was in way better shape than I was, with longer legs, too. I was huffing by the time we pushed into the dentist's office.

My mom worked there, but we wouldn't be staying long.

Or, y'know, at all.

Poof.

❖

The moment he saw where we were, Malik frowned at me.

"Why did you bring us here?" Malik said. We were outside his house, at his front door.

"Because I don't want them to hurt you."

That, apparently, wasn't the right answer. Malik scowled.

"They can do stuff," I said. "Brain-melty stuff. I told you. Go inside, and I'll get the hell out of here."

"So, what? You're gonna just keep running forever?"

"No," I said. "I'm…I'm going to try and find that woman again."

"What woman?"

"There was a woman. Lexa. I met her over waffles. Look, it doesn't matter. She said she would talk to me again. And…" I trailed off. "And maybe she can…"

"She can what?"

"I don't know!" I threw my hands up in the air. "But I don't want them to do anything to *you*."

Malik crossed his arms and took a step toward me. I didn't back away. We were standing very, very close to each other.

"Cole," he said.

I cut him off. "I just need to make a plan. I need you to go inside and be safe." I tried to hold up one hand in what little space was between us, which didn't work because instead I had my hand pressed against his forearm. Oh man. "Please, *please* just let me figure out something, and then I swear I will tell you what it is and we can figure it out from there. Okay?"

He exhaled, and I lowered my hand. "Do you even know where she is? That woman?"

I winced. "Lexa? She said she worked at a gallery. We were gonna meet up, but I kind of missed it with all the running away we were doing just now."

He blew out a breath. "Oh. Well, then. No problem."

I groaned. "I know. This is insane. But I don't know what else to do."

Malik took a deep breath and let it go, like maybe he was counting to ten in his head. "It's getting late. I don't think any galleries will be open right now. Where are you going to go?"

"Home," I said. "I can keep them out overnight, for sure."

"Are you sure you don't want me to stay with you?"

I looked at him. He was still scowling at me. His arms were still crossed, and he was really, really close. It was so unfair he looked that good while he was glaring at me, because it meant any time he glared at me I was totally going to cave. I could already feel it. I wanted him to stay with me. I was scared out of my freaking mind, I had no plan, and Malik was bigger and stronger than me. Duh. Of course I wanted him to stay.

But. If he was with me and Beardy and the Brain-Melters came back?

I shook my head. "In all the ways I may have imagined a moment like this, me turning you down was not among them. But here we are. I need to find Lexa, and I need to know you're okay while I find her. Every time I teleport, she said they can hear me. So, I want you here. Away from me. Safe."

Malik's scowl softened and faded. Then he chuckled. "You imagine me?"

I swallowed. My face burned. "Don't let it go to your head."

"Oh, it's there," he said.

"Well, there was less running for our lives, and more—" I bit off the word.

"More?" His smile grew.

I shook my head. "I'm done talking. Talking leads to death by embarrassment." I looked over his shoulder. "Please. Just stay here. I'll be okay, and I'll text you as soon as I get home. We can figure out a new plan in the morning."

"You telling me what to do?"

"Yes."

He stared at me long enough that I thought he was going to argue again, but then he nodded and turned. I couldn't decide whether to be let down or to celebrate. I wanted to do both. Malik was stubborn as hell. I walked with him to his front door, and he turned to face me again.

"Go right home," he said.

"You telling me what to do?" I said.

"Yes," he said, and then we were looking right at each other and his brown eyes were sort of everything that ever mattered. Ever.

He looked away. "Cole," he said.

Oh crap. "It's okay," I said.

"No," he said. "It's not."

I held up my hand. I so didn't want to have this conversation. Not after the night we'd just had. "I get it."

"Oh my God, shut up," he said.

I shut up.

"I like you. A lot," he said. "And that's...*big*. So, that *more* you were imagining? I've been imagining it, too. I'm just not sure I'm ready for..." He struggled for a second. "More."

I nodded. I didn't trust myself to say anything.

"Not yet," he said. "But. Yeah."

He reached behind him and opened the door to his house.

"As soon as you get home—" he said, but that's all he had time to say before I felt the tug, and two hands grabbed at Malik and pulled him backward through the doorway.

Between blinks, he was gone.

Poof.

TWENTY-FIVE

I jumped forward, but I was too late. I reached out for the feeling of the door, grabbing at the handle just before it closed. Instead of feeling the usual sensation of endless choices and the flowing tugs, it was more like running headlong into a brick wall at full tilt. I bounced bodily back out onto the front stoop, where I nearly fell over and had to spend a few seconds just breathing to clear my head. The door closed in front of me.

They'd locked it. So that's what that felt like. Ow.

Malik.

They have Malik.

"No. No no no no no." My hands were shaking. I glanced over my shoulder, convinced I'd find Beardy or Freckle-Face or Mr. Stiff waiting for me, but I was alone on the street in front of Malik's house, and Malik was gone.

Malik was gone.

I needed to...

What? What was the plan? They had him and...And...?

"Find him," I said. My voice cracked on the words. Okay, but how? They'd just locked the door in front of me.

The world is full of doors, Cole.

For a second, I considered going inside Malik's house, but I realized his folks might have already heard us. If that was the case, I needed to go. It wasn't like they could help, and what would I even say to them? Some teleporting freaks have kidnapped your kid?

Yeah. Not gonna fly.

I turned and bolted.

Every house on the street seemed to be mocking me. They all

had front doors. Surely some of them were unlocked. But if I ran up to a house and it was locked and someone heard me or saw me? What if someone called the cops? No good. I needed a way in that had no consequences. It was late. Most places would be closed.

Why hadn't I borrowed the car? Or at least ridden my bike? Ugh.

I ran. My house was farther away than downtown, and I was pretty sure at least one of the restaurants or bars would be open. By the time I hit Main Street, I was panting, and it was painfully clear I was not in good shape. The lights were on at the Inn my parents liked to go to for Date Night.

It would do.

I slowed down as I approached the Inn. It was full of people, and I was pretty sure it would draw attention if I ran up at a full tilt and then vanished. So I forced myself to look as normal as a teenager could look after running for way too long. I took a few deep breaths, ran my hands through my hair, and then walked up to the front of the Inn.

I grabbed the door handle, and the whole of everywhere on the other side latched on to me. I closed my eyes and let the terrifying sensation of being pulled in all directions at once settle down again. I was in charge, not the door.

Lexa had said she could feel me. That they all could, because I was loud.

That had to be the firework thing. I could feel little pulses out there, as though distant, tiny explosions were going off. The vibration was just now reaching my chest, but none of them felt right. None of them felt like Beardy, or Freckle-Face, or even Lexa.

The world was full of doors. And more freaks like me were out there than I'd thought. How could I possibly find the right door or the right freak, when I didn't know where they'd taken him and I wasn't even sure which freak had done the job?

The only thing I knew was Malik was out there, and they intended to take his memories from him. He'd be missing a piece of time like I was when I was a kid, and the more I thought about it, the worse it was. I'd been a kid, and it was a few hours. To be our age and lose that much time? Colenap didn't cover it. He'd be pitied and a pariah in no time.

And if they wanted to take the last two weeks from him, there was more to it. These last two freaking weeks was pretty much our entire friendship. Not to mention he'd freaking come out to me. They'd literally shove him back in the closet if they stole those memories.

No. No way. Not the plan.

My phone pinged. It was my dad again. *You're late*, it said.

Of course. Because I totally needed this. I hesitated, then typed.

So sorry. Bumped into Alec. Impromptu movie night. Might stay over, if that's okay?

I watched the little three grey dots, bouncing on the heels of my feet.

Okay.

I exhaled and did something I never do. I used my phone to call someone.

Alec picked up on the second ring. "Hey. What's up?" He sounded surprised.

"I need you to cover for me. We're having a movie night right now, okay? Just...if my parents call. If they call, just let me know, and I can be right there."

Alec didn't speak for a few long seconds. "You sound freaked."

"I am. It's a thing. It's kind of a big thing, and I can't explain it. I'm dealing, but I need some time."

Another long pause. "Okay."

"Thank you," I said. My eyes filled with tears. "Thank you. You have no idea."

"You'll tell me later," he said. It didn't sound like a request.

"I will. Thank you," I said again, and then hung up.

Okay. Parents? Check.

I flinched when I thought about Malik's parents. Jesus. He'd been kidnapped by those freaks, and they were after me and...

Wait.

I frowned, looking around. No sign of Beardy, or Freckle-Face, or Mr. Stiff.

What did that mean?

I needed someone who knew what they were doing, and that was a really short list.

I heard a noise and looked up. On the other side of the door, I could see a couple approaching through the frosted glass. How long had I been standing here? I took a deep breath.

It was like the window. I was just going to have to jump and hope I could do what I needed to do. It was a terrible plan, but it was better than no plan.

It was also all I had.

I needed help if I was going to find Malik. I knew exactly one person who might be able to make that happen.

Lexa, I thought. *Blue hair. Funny accent. Likes too much sugar in her coffee. A freak like me.*

Poof.

❖

I tumbled out the door, hit a small coffee table, and sent everything on it flying around the entranceway. Something shattered. Something else clattered. I swore. Smooth, Cole. Very smooth.

I scrambled to my feet just in time to hear a click. The light came on.

Lexa stared at me, her mouth wide open. She also had a baseball bat.

"Please don't hit me," I said.

"How...?" she said.

"How do you think?" I said. I had no time for this. "They took Malik."

She shook her head. "Who's Malik?"

"He's my..." I almost said *boyfriend*. "Friend. They grabbed him. They were chasing us all over the place, and they just snatched him from his own front doorway."

"He can teleport?" She frowned.

"No. He was just coming with me. We were hanging out. Beardy McAsshole showed up. That's why I missed our dinner date. Were you there? I'm sorry if you were there. Could you maybe put down the baseball bat?"

Lexa finally lowered the bat. "You teleported with your friend?" She didn't sound quite as angry now so much as she sounded worried.

I nodded. "I wasn't going to leave him behind. They showed up outside where he worked."

"Cole," Lexa said. "They don't want people to know about us."

"Well, too late," I said. "It's their fault he knows in the first place. The first time I escaped them, I landed in Malik's bedroom. He wasn't buying 'I jumped up two storeys to get through your window.'" I swallowed. "Where are they? Where would they take him? Are they going to melt his brain?"

Lexa frowned. She was wearing a really long T-shirt and nothing else I could see. I guess she'd been sleeping. I looked around. It seemed like a nice apartment. Small, but nice. Except for the shattered bowl. My bad.

"So you came here," she said.

"Will they listen to you?"

"It's not that simple," she said. "I'm not a part of their group. I didn't join them, exactly. I don't like a lot of what they do."

"No kidding," I said. "What with mind-melting four-year-olds."

"What?"

"They got me once already when I was a kid," I said. "How do I find them?"

"Cole."

"They took Malik!" Just like that, I was yelling. "Everything in the last two weeks? It's too important! He's...He's learned and done some *really important things* the last two weeks, okay? They can't take it. I won't let them." To my complete humiliation, my eyes were filling up.

It took her a few seconds to answer. I braced myself for another round of arguments, for another thing I could say to maybe shake her into helping me. Anything.

"Okay," she said.

My whole body went liquid with relief. I had to grab the wall to stay upright. "Okay?" I said.

She nodded. "Okay. I'm not sure what I can do, but...Okay. Look, if they just took him, we have time. They'll have to rest and...Okay. Let me get dressed. And I'm going to put on some coffee. You want some?"

I nodded. "Yes. Please. Thank you."

I followed her past a small living room into a narrow kitchen. I looked out the window and saw rows of houses, each lower than the next on a sloping road, and water beyond them. The houses were painted bright colors. I could see that, even though it was dark out, thanks to the streetlights and the moon. It was pretty clear I wasn't in Ottawa.

"So," I said. "Where am I, exactly?"

"St. John's," she said.

"Huh," I said. I wasn't sure what else to say. I'd never been to Newfoundland before. She left to go get dressed, and I stared out at the ocean, something like two thousand kilometers from where I'd just been a few minutes ago.

❖

The coffee Lexa made was really strong. I didn't complain.

"When you didn't show up to meet with me, I was worried."

"Things got a little busy. They were chasing me. Us."

"You need to understand they've got their way of doing things."

I put the mug down gently. It looked handmade. "They kidnap people and make them forget about it."

She nodded. "Yes. Can you imagine what people would do if they knew about us?"

I could. And although I could totally see her point, I wasn't about to hand over Malik just because they were paranoid about what would happen if the world found out doors weren't safe from people like me. Malik wasn't going to tell. Who would believe him? Some random guy yelling about people who teleported? Who'd care? It wasn't like he had any freaking proof.

Oh.

Oh wait.

"What?" Lexa said. She sounded worried.

I realized I was smiling. "Can you get me a meeting with them?"

She frowned. "Why?"

"I want to talk to them. I want a chance to explain without them trying to grab me or attack me or put the whammy on my brain."

Lexa was still frowning. "Cole—"

"You said we had time. How much time? Before they…Before they start on Malik."

She glanced over the clock on her microwave. She seemed to be doing some math. "At least until morning. Eight hours, I think."

"Why?" I asked, not sure if I was relieved or not I had that much time. Not even sure that it was enough time. "Why the wait?"

She held her mug in both hands. "Burying things isn't easy. I can't do it at all. Most of us can't. Unlocking something in someone that they've been hiding or denying isn't too difficult. I do it with artists all the time. It's not *invasive*. The mind wants to be open, but all the noise and anxiety and pressure keeps it shut, you know? But pushing something away and making someone *forget* is a lot of work, and it's exhausting. They won't try it until they've had a rest. If they've been chasing you, they'll be too tired."

I hoped that was true. When they'd snatched me the first time, they'd been pretty quick to try it on me, hadn't they?

But no, they hadn't. Freckle-Face had grabbed me, but Beardy hadn't tried the brain-melting until later. I'd led Beardy, Freckle-Face, and Mr. Stiff all over the place today. And Beardy seemed to be the head brain-melter.

"Is it just the three of them?"

Lexa nodded. "For this sort of thing? Usually. They handle this kind of trouble in our area, anyway."

"Area."

"This continent. North America."

Well. That was…information.

"Okay," I said. "I want a meeting. In the morning, before they even think of trying anything on Malik. I want to plead my case."

"I can try." Lexa took another swallow of her coffee.

"Okay. So, that's the plan. You get them to agree to meet with me. I'll give you my number. Text me when you know where I should go."

She looked surprised. "You're not staying put?"

"Nope. I'll go home. Get ready." I shrugged. "I don't think they're going to chase me now they've got Malik. I think that was the whole point. Do something I couldn't run away from."

"Probably." Lexa nodded. I didn't like that she agreed with me, but there it was. "What are you going to say to them?"

"Whatever I have to."

"Cole," Lexa said, then she seemed not to want to say anything else.

"Yeah?"

"I don't want you to think…I'm not…" She blew out a breath. "I'm not sure what you can expect from them."

"Yeah," I said. "But what else can I do?"

As plans went? It wasn't the best.

Luckily, I had a few hours.

And more importantly, I had my phone.

Lexa nodded. She looked really unhappy. I couldn't say I blamed her.

"Text me when you're ready," I said, making for Lexa's front door. I didn't even finish my coffee.

St. John's, Newfoundland, and I were through for the night.

But I had one hell of a to-do list.

TWENTY-SIX

I'd barely finished and had just hit the Enter key on my laptop when my phone pinged. I'd put Lexa down as "Lexa Blue" since I didn't know her actual name, and my stomach clenched when I saw the message.

They've agreed to meet with you. Can you meet me at my place? We can go together.

Something about having her come with me made me feel just slightly better.

I looked at the clock. It was five in the morning, and after everything I'd been up to, I was wrecked. This was the worst plan ever. It involved none of my strengths, and I had exactly one move in my arsenal. Oh my God, I was going to end up with my brain melted, drooling in a corner, wasn't I?

Stop. Just stop. The voice in my head sounded an awful lot like Nat. *There's one goal: Malik.*

I exhaled, unplugged my phone, and tapped out a response.

Be right there.

A moment later, I was back in St. John's, Newfoundland. Sunlight streamed in the windows.

Lexa was holding out a cup of coffee when I stepped into her hallway. She'd changed into a nice sleeveless black blouse and capris, and her eyes were back to that sharp look she did with her makeup. She looked together, in all senses of the word.

I felt grubby and tired and gritty just looking at her. I wanted to sleep for a thousand years.

"Thanks," I said. The cup was handmade, painted in earth tones. I took a big swallow, ignoring how my hand was shaking. When was the last time I'd had this much coffee?

Never. Never was the last time.

"Okay," I said. "Where are we going?"

"You can come with me," Lexa said, reaching out her hand. I took it. Now both of us were ignoring how much my hand was shaking. It was nice of her to play along.

I put the pretty cup on the table in the entrance hall. Lexa reached out for the door. The moment she touched it, the possibility of everywhere thrummed through me. Even in the last few hours, it had gotten all the clearer to me. *This way to the Louvre. This way to Parliament. This way to home.*

"Do you ever get used to that feeling?" I asked.

Lexa's small smile was answer enough.

"Ready?" she said.

"Not even a little," I said.

She nodded and opened the door.

❖

Wherever we were, it was expensive and old. The door we'd come through led into a ballroom or something. Super-tall windows covered in heavy curtains lined one wall, and the floor was some kind of really shiny rock. Marble, I supposed. It reminded me of the Château Laurier, but I didn't think that was where we were. The opulent room was longer than it was wide, and along the wall opposite the covered windows were probably a half-dozen doors. We'd come through one at the end.

The room had no furniture unless you counted really big chandeliers and art mounted in thick wooden frames. I briefly wondered if I might be in the Louvre—which would have been hysterical, in a terrible way—but I didn't recognize any of the pieces or see any security cameras.

That didn't mean there weren't any. I just knew the cameras at the Louvre were in plain sight.

We were alone.

"Are we early?" I said. I realized I was still holding Lexa's hand, and I let go.

The other doors started to open. I could feel the pull-and-release in my chest with every opening and closing. I didn't recognize the first man—he was older, balding and grey—but the second man was Freckle-Face. He wasn't alone.

Malik was with him.

I took a step forward, but Lexa touched my elbow and I stopped. Malik saw me. "Cole," he said.

"Hey," I said. I waved. Wow. Even faced with a room full of teleporting freaks, I could find a way to make it awkward.

And it *was* full. The doors were still opening.

Malik looked okay. I mean, as much as it was possible to tell across the room and at a glance, anyway. He didn't look brain-melted. That was good.

Speaking of brain-melting, Beardy McBeardface arrived. I glared at him. He didn't seem to care.

The group of freaks arranged themselves into a semicircle. They were facing Lexa and me with pretty bland expressions on their faces. It was so surreal. These people had just teleported here from wherever the hell they'd been, bringing my kidnapped friend with them, and they stood around like it was a boring suit convention and someone was about to start suggesting the first topic be whether or not they should consider allowing bow ties.

Lexa was one of four women out of the two dozen people gathered. That didn't feel like a good omen, either.

Also? The suits did nothing for them.

"Mr. Cole Tozer," said one of the men. It wasn't Beardy or Freckle-Face. It was the older man who'd been the first to arrive.

"Yes," I said, because I felt like I needed to say something.

"I understand you have something you wish to say to us?"

I swallowed.

"I want you to let Malik go. No melting his brain. Just let him go." The man's eyebrows rose. Both of them. "That's it?"

"Well, I'd really appreciate not having my brain melted, too, and maybe not having this guy show up every time I turn around." I pointed at Beardy.

He flinched.

Huh. Beardy wasn't the big fish in the room. If anything, his particular subset of freaks seemed to be at the bottom of whatever pecking order was in play. He stood at the back of the semicircle and kept his hands behind his back. Deferential, maybe, or just hiding nerves.

I glanced at Malik. Freckle-Face still had his hand on Malik's shoulder, but Malik met my gaze. I was afraid. Malik, though?

He looked *pissed.*

Something about that gave me a bit more courage.

"That's what I want," I said. It came out stronger. It didn't sound like a request.

The man regarded me. He had pale eyes and didn't blink much. I managed not to blink or look away.

"Cole," he started, then paused. "May I call you Cole?"

"Okay."

"Cole," he said again. "We have a problem." His intense eyes finally left mine and glanced over at Malik. "Or, more to the point, we have two problems."

I waited for him to look at me again.

"I've pretty much got a handle on the teleporting thing now," I said. I hated how much it sounded like I wanted his approval, but the truth was I did. Hell, I needed it. I needed this creepy old man in a suit to decide I wasn't a threat.

"It's not that," the man said, smiling. It wasn't a good smile. He smiled the way Austin smiled: like he was looking at something beneath his notice, which amused him.

Lexa was right. These guys were assholes.

"Okay," I said. It wasn't okay.

"We have an order to things," he said. "And you're…early. We also keep the strictest of confidences, and…" He gestured to Malik without looking at him. His body language was pretty clear: *You screwed up, Cole.*

"So you want to take away my teleporting," I said. "Like you did last time."

For the first time, the old man looked surprised. And he wasn't the only one. A ripple of motion seemed to travel through the room. A shifting of a stance. The twitch of a shoulder. Tiny things, but people spoke with their bodies all the time.

I was seeing discomfort. Surprise. Annoyance.

"Yes," the old man said, drawing the word out a bit. He sounded like a snake. "You're aware of that?"

"I figured it out," I said. "It would have been way better if you'd dropped me off back home, by the way. Just saying."

He waved that off. "We couldn't have a child muse."

There was that word again. Muse.

"I get that," I said. "But I'm not a child."

"We prefer our members wait beyond their teenage years," he said. It almost sounded like an apology. Almost.

And here it was. I took a deep breath. I met Malik's gaze for a second. He still looked pissed.

"Fine," I said. "Go ahead."

The whole room looked at me.

"Cole?" Lexa said. She touched my arm again.

I wanted to look at Malik again, but I didn't dare. As it was, I wasn't sure I'd manage to keep my voice from breaking. "You can take it. Or lock it. Bury it. Whatever. I won't fight you if you want to take away my teleporting thing, but you don't touch any memories. Not mine, and not his," I said, looking at Malik.

"Cole," the old man started, but I held up my hand.

"Not done. You're not putting him back in the closet. Do you hear me? We walk out of here with our memories."

"I'm not sure you understand the gravity of the situation."

"I understand you want this kept a secret. Fine." I raised my hands. "You let us keep our memories, and I won't tell. I won't resist."

"Cole—"

"But if you try melting my brain, *resisting* won't be the half of it. The whole damn world will learn about you guys, and I promise enough people will see me pop in and out of doors around the world that you could melt brains for the next nine months and you *still* wouldn't get everyone. How many people do you think visit the Louvre every day? How many cameras? Someone walking the world, door to fucking door, for everyone to see? What do you think that'll do to your creepy suit clique? You so much as *try* to mess with his head, we'll all find out."

"We'd never allow that to happen," Beardy McBeardface said. Man, I hated him. "What makes you think you'd even make it to a door?"

"Dude. I'm a planner." I smiled at him and held up my phone. "This isn't a to-do list. *It's already done*. I don't have to make it out the door. If I don't go home *tonight* and click some buttons? It's everywhere."

Beardy frowned.

"Tumblr. Twitter. You've heard of social media, right? It's a pretty big thing these days."

His eyes widened.

I waved my phone again. "I'm not the best cameraman, but I think people will care more about the locations than the story. Everywhere I went, there were cameras. If there were people, I talked to them. I told them my name. I even asked them to take my picture. Time zones are pretty cool, and some places have people all hours of the day. If I don't go home with Malik? Well, it might not be as good as me streaking in Parliament on a live feed—I am *totally* prepared to do that, too, by the way—but I bet you're just as screwed if my video gets out and I can't tell anyone how I did it because you melted my brain. All those cameras? They have time stamps. All those other people? They'll remember the goofy Canadian kid. And no one will be able to explain how I was in Paris and London and Rome and all those other places in a few hours." I paused. "Also, the *Mona Lisa* is really small. Like, it's tiny. Did you guys know that?"

Now they weren't just looking at me, they were wide-eyed. Some had their mouths open.

"I'm running on coffee and anger, and I've got finals on Monday. I'm *so* done with you people." I pointed at Beardy. "Don't blame me. Blame him. And stop threatening me. If you block the doors, I'll use a fucking window."

"He can do it," Lexa said. "This kid's a prodigy. That's how good he is."

I blinked, looking at Lexa. I was a what-now? "What?"

She smiled. "Most of us can't go somewhere we've never been unless we follow each other. Ride the echo."

It clicked. "Like the diner?" I said. She'd found me at the diner. She'd said I was "loud." She'd shown up right after I got there.

She nodded. "You're talented, Cole. *Way* beyond these guys. You got to my place hours after the last time I used my door. They couldn't do that. You did."

"Alexis," Beardy said.

"Don't call me that," Lexa said. "And frown all you want, Michael. It won't make it any less true. That kid is better than you. Than *all* of you." She smiled.

"The very fact he's making those threats shows us he's not responsible enough to be trusted," the old man said, taking the conversation back from Beardy—Michael.

"Oh, bullshit," Lexa said. "We *all* travel wherever we want. Don't suggest he's any different than the rest of us. This isn't his fault, it's yours. Your rules. Michael attacked him. Michael kidnapped his friend. That's a *felony*, Richard."

The old man—Richard—sighed, as though felonies were the least of his worries.

"He's already doing things it took the rest of us months to figure out, and if Alexis is right, he's done things most of us will never be able to do," another man said. "Is it worth the risk?"

"Is it worth the risk to piss him off?" Lexa said. "I don't think you *could* lock his gift, even if you wanted to. Not even you, Michael. He's stronger than you. You've already handled everything wrong. Maybe someone should try treating him like a human being. You'd be surprised how much that helps."

"She's right," I said. "I'm totally good with that."

"We can't let him—" Michael started.

"Shut up, Michael," Richard said.

Michael stuttered to a stop. Everyone stopped talking.

"You can retract your...plan?"

I checked my phone. "So long as I'm home in time, sure. I just have to unschedule the posts."

"You'll agree to a mentor?"

"Richard," Michael said.

The old man just held up his hand. Didn't even look at Beardy. *Burn.*

"As long as it's Lexa, sure," I said.

The old man looked at me for a few long breaths. I looked right back. *Tick-tock, old man.*

"We're done here," he said.

Michael looked like he wanted to say more, but he didn't. He nodded at Freckle-Face, who let go of Malik. I met him halfway, before I even really realized I'd started walking.

"Hey," I said.

"Hey," he said.

"Take them home," Richard said.

"I'm good," I said. "I've got this." I glanced at Lexa, who nodded and gestured to the door we'd come in through.

I held out my hand, and Malik took it. Both of us were shaking, but neither of us let it show on our faces. I led him to the door.

"I'll text you," Lexa said. "About setting up some time to get together."

"That'd be great. Maybe give me a couple of weeks for exams first?"

She nodded.

I led Malik through the door.

Poof.

❖

Outside Malik's house, standing on his front steps, I turned to face him.

"Are you okay?" I said. My voice wobbled, and my stomach was flipping. Anger and caffeine were completely tapping out.

He nodded slowly, looking around like he couldn't believe we were back at his house. "I can't believe you did that."

I blinked. "Did what?"

"You were going to let them take it from you," he said. "You were going to let them just…" He shook his head.

"They were going to make you forget everything," I said. "Two whole weeks. I lost an afternoon to them when I was a kid, and it was awful enough. Trust me. Not recommended."

He was staring again. His gaze locked me in place. "More," he said.

I didn't follow. More? More what? "Pardon?"

He reached out with both hands and put them on my shoulders. Then he gave me a little tug, and I took a half step forward. He leaned in, with a slow and easy smile that didn't at all cover the nervousness in his eyes. I didn't know what to do with my hands. I ended up putting them against his chest. He was warm through his T-shirt, and felt really, really real.

"Ah," I said. "*More.*"

For a guy who'd never kissed another guy before, Malik sure didn't mind being in charge. I had to kind of scoot up on my toes because he was so tall, but his aim was on target and he definitely had skills. Who knew a kiss could make my whole body go all wobbly and also very not wobbly all at the same time?

Louis had nothing on this guy.

My eyes were closed. I didn't remember doing that, but when Malik finally pulled away a few seconds later, and after our first kiss had become a second, third, and maybe even a fourth kiss, I realized it and opened my eyes.

He was smiling again.

"What?" I said.

"Streaking in Parliament, eh? Bullet, you're a wild man."

"Listen," I said. "I'm new to this whole making-threats-up-on-the-fly thing, and—"

He interrupted me with kiss number five, repeating until somewhere in the double digits, when I finally lost track and stopped counting.

And that was how his mom found us when she opened the front door.

Like I said, there is no good moment I cannot find a way to make awkward.

EPILOGUE

If anyone ever asks me for proof of how unfair the world is, I won't be able to tell the truth. But if I could, I'd say: Unfair is being grounded for a week because you rescued the cutest guy in school from brain-melting freaks and can't tell anyone that's why you blew curfew.

No plan in existence covered why, from his parents' point of view, Malik hadn't gone home from work and was out all night without calling. Especially when he ended up on his front porch making out with some guy. Plus side? Malik's parents didn't flip out about the bi thing. Not at all. If anything, maybe it played to his advantage a little bit because they got it in their heads that he somehow felt he couldn't talk to them, and it had gotten all teary and super super awkward.

Because I'd been there, too, waiting for my parents to drive over after Malik's mom had called them. Given that I was supposed to have been at Alec's house, not only did Malik end up grounded, but so did I.

Plus side? No one had checked in with Alec, so he hadn't lied to cover me or he would have probably been grounded, too.

So, that whole scene had truly sucked.

I mean, not the kissing. The kissing had been pretty awesome, but all the stuff that came after, with the angry parents. Especially when my mom and Malik's mom started talking, which was, well...It involved super-super-invasive questions from my mom about *things* I might have been *doing*, and my plan is to repress every word she spoke until my dying day.

And that was before my dad got involved with the questions. Ever been grilled by a professional body-language reader?

Seriously. Super invasive.

Anyway. Five days down, two to go. Also, as of ten minutes ago when I handed in my last exam, I was done with high school. I never had to care about calculus ever again.

Malik found me by the tree. It had become our spot over the last week. He walked up, giving me a little wave, and then sat down beside me.

"Done," he said.

"Yep," I said. "You know, two weeks ago exams seemed way more important."

"No kidding."

I looked around. We were alone on the field. I reached out and took his hand.

He squeezed back.

"So," he said. "What now?"

"I have no idea." I blew out a breath. I didn't have my bullet journal with me. It was at home. That was a new plan for the summer. Or lack of one. Something like that. "I'm thinking of taking a gap year."

He leaned away. "Really?"

"Yeah. Really. I hear it's a good plan. Lets you explore things. But if I do go to school, I'm thinking I'm going to take an art class or two. See if I can minor in graphic design, maybe. I don't know. Something with drawing."

Malik smiled, then he got up and lifted me up onto my feet. "That's cool. But that's not what I meant. I meant right now. What are you doing after school right now?"

"Oh. Same answer. No idea." I smiled. Look at me. I was getting the hang of being spontaneous. "And that's okay."

"Would you like to maybe do that together?" He said it all casual like, but he didn't look at me. It was adorable. We started back for the school.

"In case you forgot, we're grounded."

"I didn't forget. But we've got an hour before the buses come. We can hang out. And there's always next week. When we're not grounded."

That was true.

"Sure," I said. "Did you want to see who else is free?" I knew Rhonda had her last exam right now, too. I wasn't sure about anyone else.

"No." The firmness in his response made me look. He stopped and faced me. "I'd like it to be us."

"Wait." Something in my chest did a couple of little flips. "Is this a date? Are you asking me out on a date? A week ahead?"

Malik did his little look-away-and-smile thing. "Maybe. I know you like to have time to plan."

"That's cheating," I said. But every little bit of me warmed up, from head to toe. I was grinning. I'm sure there's a cool, calm, and collected way to react to the news the hottie is asking you out on a date, but I didn't know it. I may have done an air-punch. There might have been whoops. The only witnesses were me and the aforementioned hottie in question, and it didn't need to go any farther.

We started walking again, crossing the field.

"That's a yes?" Malik, on the other hand, knew how to do cool and calm and collected, though unless I was mistaken, he had a serious grin fighting to make it to the surface. "And can I book you for sometime next week, once we're not grounded?"

"That is *so* a yes." I paused. "Well, depending on where you want to go. No sportsball. But other than that? Yes. What do you want to do?"

Malik shook his head. "Nuh-uh. You pick. I just used up all the guts I had to ask you out, Bullet."

Bullet. I was never going to be tired of that nickname. Ever. We were almost at the front doors, which was when it hit me.

New plan. Spontaneity and I weren't exactly close, but I'd give it a shot and see if we could get along. I mean, Malik was right. We had an hour.

A whole hour.

I pulled out my phone and set an alarm for forty-five minutes. I might have been turning over a new leaf, but I wasn't completely abandoning my organized ways.

"Pick a number," I said.

"What?" Malik said, frowning at the screen.

"One to five," I said. I tapped the phone, starting the timer.

He took a second. "Three."

I held out my hand. He barely hesitated, taking it and smiling at me. Oh man, this boy. I was doomed.

I tried to remember our conversation. Vimy was first. And then London? What had been third? Oh! Right. Well, I'd seen photos. That was enough. Like Lexa said, I was a freaking prodigy of the teleporting freaks.

"I hear the beignets are awesome," I said.

I saw it in his eyes the moment he got it. Now he did grin. A big, goofy, delighted grin that made his whole face light up. I wanted to be the guy who made him do that every time.

"Really?" he said.

I reached out and opened the door to the school.

"Really."

Poof.

About the Author

'Nathan Burgoine grew up a reader and studied literature in university while making a living as a bookseller. His first published short story was "Heart" in the collection *Fool for Love: New Gay Fiction*. This began his long love affair with short fiction, which has seen dozens more short stories published. Even though short fiction is his favorite, 'Nathan stepped into novel writing, and his first novel, *Light*, was a finalist for a Lambda Literary Award. *Triad Blood* and *Triad Soul* are available now from Bold Strokes Books, and more novels as well as works of short fiction are always under way.

A cat lover, 'Nathan managed to fall in love with and marry Daniel, who is a confirmed dog person. Their ongoing "cat or dog" détente ended with the rescue of a husky named Coach. They live in Ottawa, Canada, where most of the time they play board games and RPGs like the geeky gaymer nerds they are.

Books Available From Bold Strokes Books

Death Checks In by David S. Pederson. Despite Heath's promises to Alan to not get involved, Heath can't resist investigating a shopkeeper's murder in Chicago, which dashes their plans for a romantic weekend getaway. (978-1-163555-329-1)

Exit Plans for Teenage Freaks by 'Nathan Burgoine. Cole always has a plan—especially for escaping his small-town reputation as "that kid who was kidnapped when he was four"—but when he teleports to a museum, it's time to face facts: it's possible he's a total freak after all. (978-1-163555-098-6)

Of Echoes Born by 'Nathan Burgoine. A collection of queer fantasy short stories set in Canada from Lambda Literary Award finalist 'Nathan Burgoine. (978-1-63555-096-2)

The Lurid Sea by Tom Cardamone. Cursed to spend eternity on his knees, Nerites is having the time of his life. (978-1-62639-911-2)

Sinister Justice by Steve Pickens. When a vigilante targets citizens of Jake Finnigan's hometown, Jake and his partner Sam fall under suspicion themselves as they investigate the murders. (978-1-63555-094-8)

Club Arcana: Operation Janus by Jon Wilson. Wizards, demons, Elder Gods: Who knew the universe was so crowded, and that they'd all be out to get Angus McAslan? (978-1-62639-969-3)

Triad Soul by 'Nathan Burgoine. Luc, Anders, and Curtis—vampire, demon, and wizard—must use their powers of blood, soul, and magic to defeat a murderer determined to turn their city into a battlefield. (978-1-62639-863-4)

Gatecrasher by Stephen Graham King. Aided by a high-tech thief, the Maverick Heart crew race against time to prevent a cadre of savage corporate mercenaries from seizing control of a revolutionary wormhole technology. (978-1-62639-936-5)

Wicked Frat Boy Ways by Todd Gregory. Beta Kappa brothers Brandon Benson and Phil Connor play an increasingly dangerous game of love, seduction, and emotional manipulation. (978-1-62639-671-5)

Death Goes Overboard by David S. Pederson. Heath Barrington and Alan Keyes are two sides of a steamy love triangle as they encounter gangsters, con men, murder, and more aboard an old lake steamer. (978-1-62639-907-5)

A Careful Heart by Ralph Josiah Bardsley. Be careful what you wish for…love changes everything. (978-1-62639-887-0)

Worms of Sin by Lyle Blake Smythers. A haunted mental asylum turned drug treatment facility exposes supernatural detective Finn M'Coul to an outbreak of murderous insanity, a strange parasite, and ghosts that seek sex with the living. (978-1-62639-823-8)

Tartarus by Eric Andrews-Katz. When Echidna, Mother of all Monsters, escapes from Tartarus and into the modern world, only an Olympian has the power to oppose her. (978-1-62639-746-0)

Rank by Richard Compson Sater. Rank means nothing to the heart, but the Air Force isn't as impartial. Every airman learns that rank has its privileges. What about love? (978-1-62639-845-0)

The Grim Reaper's Calling Card by Donald Webb. When Katsuro Tanaka begins investigating the disappearance of a young nurse, he discovers more missing persons, and they all have one thing in common: The Grim Reaper Tarot Card. (978-1-62639-748-4)

Smoldering Desires by C.E. Knipes. Evan McGarrity has found the man of his dreams in Sebastian Tantalos. When an old boyfriend from Sebastian's past enters the picture, Evan must fight for the man he loves. (978-1-62639-714-9)

Tallulah Bankhead Slept Here by Sam Lollar. A coming of age/coming out story, set in El Paso of 1967, that tells of Aaron's adventures with movie stars, cool cars, and topless bars. (978-1-62639-710-1)

Death Came Calling by Donald Webb. When private investigator Katsuro Tanaka is hired to look into the death of a high-profile lawyer, he becomes embroiled in a case of murder and mayhem. (978-1-60282-979-4)

The City of Seven Gods by Andrew J. Peters. In an ancient city of aerie temples, a young priest and a barbarian mercenary struggle to refashion their lives after their worlds are torn apart by betrayal. (978-1-62639-775-0)

Lysistrata Cove by Dena Hankins. Jack and Eve navigate the maelstrom of their darkest desires and find love by transgressing gender, dominance, submission, and the law on the crystal blue Caribbean Sea. (978-1-62639-821-4)

Garden District Gothic by Greg Herren. Scotty Bradley has to solve a notorious thirty-year-old unsolved murder that has terrible repercussions in the present. (978-1-62639-667-8)

The Man on Top of the World by Vanessa Clark. Jonathan Maxwell falling in love with Izzy Rich, the world's hottest glam rock superstar, is not only unpredictable but complicated when a bold teenage fan-girl changes everything. (978-1-62639-699-9)

The Orchard of Flesh by Christian Baines. With two hotheaded men under his roof including his werewolf lover, a vampire tries to solve an increasingly lethal mystery while keeping Sydney's supernatural factions from the brink of war. (978-1-62639-649-4)

The Thassos Confabulation by Sam Sommer. With the inheritance of a great deal of money, David and Chris also inherit a nondescript brown paper parcel and a strange and perplexing letter that sends David on a quest to understand its meaning. (978-1-62639-665-4)

The Photographer's Truth by Ralph Josiah Bardsley. Silicon Valley tech geek Ian Baines gets more than he bargained for on an unexpected journey of self-discovery through the lustrous nightlife of Paris. (978-1-62639-637-1)